DEAD
INSIDER

DEAD
INSIDER

A Loon Lake Mystery

VICTORIA HOUSTON

Victoria Houston

TYRUS
BOOKS

F+W Media, Inc.

Published by
TYRUS BOOKS
an imprint of F+W Media, Inc.
10151 Carver Road, Suite 200, Blue Ash, Ohio 45242
www.tyrusbooks.com

Hardcover ISBN 10: 1-4405-6218-0
Hardcover ISBN 13: 978-1-4405-6218-1
Trade Paperback ISBN 10: 1-4405-3356-3
Trade Paperback ISBN 13: 978-1-4405-3356-3
eISBN 10: 1-4405-6213-X
eISBN 13: 978-1-4405-6213-6

Printed in the United States of America.

10 9 8 7 6 5 4 3 2 1

This book is available at quantity discounts for bulk purchases.
For information, please call 1-800-289-0963.

For Nicole and John

Also Available in the Loon Lake Mystery Series:

"Loathing is endless. Hate is a bottomless cup;
I pour and pour."

—Medea; *Medea*

Chapter One

Watching from the window on her right, Jane Ericsson stared down as the Challenger jet circled the landing strip. How many times had she flown into Loon Lake since she was a kid? A thousand times, at least. Yet she still could not tell which lake was which.

Big ones, little ones, potholes, peninsulas, and islands she should recognize but couldn't. Then again, the town of Loon Lake had over 300 lakes within a five-mile radius. So much water. So many trees. So many reasons to call this land "God's Country."

And if she won this election? Her father would be so proud. He might forgive her, his only child, for being a girl. *Too bad he isn't alive—*

The jet landed with a thud on the airstrip, sloshing her drink onto her lap. She brushed the liquid off her slacks with a distracted air. It was her third bourbon, and the first two had taken effect, so it was no great loss.

"Hey, you guys, take it easy next time, will you?" she said in a voice loud enough to carry to the cockpit. "Dry cleaning is not one of my reimbursable election expenses."

"Sorry, JT," said Curt, calling her by her childhood nickname. He had been her late father's pilot, and had known her since she was a teenager. A surrogate big brother, Curt knew the family secrets and had still been willing to help her out—a demanding flight schedule for a man in his late sixties.

"We got winds gusting to sixty miles per hour," said Curt. "Should be a lot better flying tomorrow. See you back here at ten-thirty, right? You take care driving home, you hear? The forecast shows another severe thunderstorm moving in from the west—could hit any minute."

"I'll be fine. All I need is a good night's sleep," said Jane with a sigh as she reached for her purse and briefcase. "We did great this week, guys. What did we manage, eighteen appearances in the last four days?"

She sighed again as she fumbled her way down the narrow stairs to the concrete runway. What had she been thinking when she'd decided to run for the Senate seat her father had once held? Today a senatorial race required three to four times as many appearances as when the old man ran; he'd had it easy, thirty years ago. That was before the age of YouTube and the 24/7 news cycle. This race was costing her millions to reach voters, not to mention every hour of her every day.

As she hurried across the airstrip and through the gate leading to the parking area for the owners of private planes, a sheet of warm rain hit her face. She wrenched open the door to her Jeep and clambered inside just as hail hammered the roof. Whew! They had landed just in time.

She was reaching to throw her briefcase onto the floor in front of the passenger seat when a knock on the driver's side window caught her attention. Curt, still in his pilot's gear, gestured at her. She hit the window button, letting the rain blow in. "What now?"

"Just want to be sure that you're okay to drive. I can drop you off if you want. Brad is happy to follow us if . . . if you're as tired as I think you are."

"And you're getting drenched standing there. Thanks, Curt, but no, I'm fine," she said, making sure she didn't slur any words. "See you boys in the morning."

With a wave, he ran off. Before putting her key in the ignition, Jane turned around to check the rear compartment of the car. She did not need another unpleasant surprise. It was a month since she had walked into her dark garage and strapped herself into the driver's seat only to have the sudden sense that someone—or some thing—was in the car.

She would never forget what she had seen. Forcing herself to turn around, she had confronted a mound of debris: thousands of her campaign posters had been chopped to bits and crammed into the back of the Jeep. Nor were the posters just slashed: the intruder had taken the time to carve a large black X across every photo of her face . . . and her face was on every poster.

Somewhere, somehow, the vandal had managed to steal the posters and deface each one before slicing it up. Whoever it was then lay in wait to hide the hideous results in her car. It wasn't the cost of the ruined posters that bothered her; it was the hate that must have fueled the act that she found frightening. Who could be so angry with her that they would do such a thing?

She knew from observing her father's campaigns that politics, like religion, could trigger strange and powerful emotions in people. And so it was that not a day had gone by since the chilling discovery of the vandalized posters that she didn't search the faces of the people attending her political rallies, watching for the one person who might stand too close, stare too long, or rant too loudly. So far, though, nothing more had happened.

She was grateful to one of the young staffers in the Loon Lake campaign office who had taken the time to thoroughly clean and vacuum the car so that only the memory remained. Jane sighed. Just thinking about the campaign office added to her fatigue.

What is this pesky issue with campaign funds? The accountant is sure someone is pilfering money from the campaign account, but Lauren thinks he's nuts. She insists that she's got everything under control. Given that Lauren has been doing a great job managing the entire campaign, it's likely she has a better handle on that situation than the accountant does. With eight offices now open across the state, Lauren has the better opportunity to track who is doing what and for how much. At any rate, that's one problem that can wait until Monday.

Tonight, with the back seat down, it was easy to see into cargo compartment: no weird luggage left on board. She turned the key in the ignition, slipped the car into gear, and backed out slowly. The combination of a driving rain against the glare of her headlights made it difficult to see.

Once on the highway, visibility was better. She relaxed. Thoughts of the coming day made her smile. Chuck Winters had organized a pontoon party on Lake Monona for the donors to her Thousand Dollar Club. Chuck had already arranged for donations totaling well over a hundred thousand, and now he was giving her the party . . . and more. She liked his idea of "more"—especially since he had implied that the current Mrs. Charles Winters was soon to be history.

Plus, she liked Madison. *Interesting people, great restaurants—should be a fun weekend.*

Pulling into the driveway and hitting the button to open the garage door, she planned ahead: pack for the morning, then change into her pj's, another drink—or two. And bed.

The garage door didn't move, stuck again. *Screw it*, thought Jane, *the car needs a wash anyway.*

She was awakened by a rustling in the kitchen and checked the time on her alarm clock. Oh man, it was only ten-fifteen. She lay listening. *Damn mice. Kaye must have forgotten to put out traps. Oh, that's right, Kaye isn't helping me any more. Who's that new guy Lauren hired? Did he forget to put out traps?*

More rustling. Okay, maybe she could shoo 'em out the kitchen door. Better than letting the critters find their way into her bedroom.

She threw back the coverlet, reached for her robe, and staggered down the hall toward the kitchen. Her head did not feel good—one too many bourbons.

Jane blinked against the glare of the kitchen lights: the mouse seemed as tall as a person, its head in shadow. She blinked again. Double vision didn't help. The mouse swung, and a jet plane hit her temple.

Chapter Two

"Hey, bud, am I late for breakfast?" After knocking twice, Osborne pulled open the screen door and walked through the jaws of a giant neon green muskie.

While it might appear that Dr. Paul Osborne, retired dentist, widowed father of two and grandfather to three, was about to become a piscatorial treat, it was an illusion. The huge fish was a painting that adorned the entire length of his neighbor's house trailer.

Breakfast, however, was no illusion. Earlier that Saturday morning, as a summer rain murmured outside, the smell of bacon frying had drifted up through the pines to where Osborne's kitchen windows were open and susceptible. But while he was indeed hungry for one of Ray Pradt's cosmically delicious and guaranteed cholesterol-elevating meals, he was also on a mission.

"Come on in, Doc. You are as welcome as the flowers," said Ray from the stove where his six-foot, six-inch frame was hunkered over a cast-iron frying pan. "Got Nueske's bacon, fresh eggs from the farmer's market, and some loverly . . . *loverly* raspberries, picked by yours truly."

"*Wild* raspberries?" asked Osborne, wondering if Ray would fess up to his penchant for poaching. Fish, berries, or wild game: in Ray's world, food always tasted better if it came from private property. "Private" meaning not his, not public, either—and that went for land or water.

"Wild are the best," said Ray with a wink.

"Wild keeps you out of jail is more like it," said Osborne in a dry tone as he plucked a fat berry from the bowl on the kitchen table. "Yum, ripe to perfection." He reached for another. He refused to speculate on whose berry patch Ray might have raided that morning, likely before dawn.

"Oops, I'm leaving a puddle on your floor," said Osborne. He walked back through the modest living room, past the antique phone booth with its equally antique but functional landline, to open the screen door and shake the rain off his poncho before hanging it on an antler of the deer mount that Ray used as a coat rack.

Returning to the kitchen, he stepped behind Ray to pour himself a mug of hot coffee from the coffeemaker on the counter, then walked back to pull out a chair at the kitchen table. Before he could cross his right leg over his left, Ray asked, "Doc?"

Osborne glanced over to find Ray watching him with a question in his eyes and two large brown eggs clutched in his right hand, poised over the frying pan. "One or two?"

"By all means, two, please," said Osborne. With one flick of the wrist, two eggs plopped into the hot bacon grease. "Ray, I came down to ask a favor," said Osborne as he reached for another berry. "Boy, these are good."

"Ask . . . and ye shall receive. "When Ray was in good humor, his speech pattern could hold his audience hostage to the point of tears.

"I could use a nice catch of walleye for dinner tonight—"

"Sure, and . . . what time did you want to go? All this rain—it rained like hell all night, and it just keeps on coming. The client I had booked for the day canceled last night. Wife's making him go shopping."

"Well, I was hoping not to go out in the boat myself," said Osborne.

Ray's eyebrows rose." Are you upset with me or something?"

"Gosh, no. Mallory is driving up from Chicago this morning with that new guy she's been seeing. Some executive she met at the office. I promised her I'd put together a classic Northwoods dinner this evening. When I suggested the walleye and said I was pretty sure you could help me out, she told me to include you."

"Really? You sure about that?"

"And you may bring a guest should you so wish. My suggestion being female, educated—you know what I mean—someone who'll fit in."

"Now . . . why the dickens would you say something like that?" Ray looked over at him with a sly smile.

"You know why." Osborne had learned the hard way that unless otherwise instructed, Ray had a habit of showing up with some real conversation stoppers: fellows who lived down roads with no fire numbers. Good at heart, short on teeth.

He was aware, too, that Ray had just broken up with a woman he'd been seeing until her husband got wind of it. Given that situation. Osborne figured it was highly unlikely Ray would arrive with a member of the opposite sex, which suited Osborne fine. The challenge of the evening would be best met if Ray came alone.

"Okay." That was all Ray said as he dropped two slices of bread into the toaster on the counter to his right, then eased Osborne's eggs over with a touch as light as when he slipped the hook from the mouth of a fish without a tear in the delicate membrane.

When the eggs were done to over-easy perfection, he reached overhead for a warmed plate onto which he scooped the eggs, added two slices of bacon, and popped the bread up from the toaster. Not a gesture was wasted, nor another word spoken.

Watching his friend, Osborne wondered if the not-so-distant history between Mallory, his eldest daughter, and Ray had anything to do with his silence. Maybe Osborne's invitation was a mistake, and Ray would rather not come to dinner with Mallory's new friend? Maybe he should go and buy some shrimp instead? It was about this same time two years ago, not long after her divorce, that Mallory had driven north nearly every weekend, and did not sleep in her own bedroom. For a time Osborne had worried that Ray might be his next son-in-law. He loved the guy, but thank the Lord it hadn't happened. The affair was over by hunting season, and the two appeared to have reached a comfortable détente: friends, not lovers. But given Ray's silence, maybe Osborne was asking too much. "Lew will be there too," said Osborne. "Be just the five of us. But if you have plans . . ." Still no response. "I'm sorry," he said. "I just thought . . . well, in some ways you know Mallory better than I do. She said she wants our opinions on this guy—"

"You sure about that?" said Ray, filling his own plate and bringing it over to the table.

Osborne nodded. "Yes, but I understand if you're not comfortable. Forget the fish, I'll stop by the market for some shrimp."

"Don't do that, Doc. I was just thinking . . . you said I can bring a guest, right?" Ray reached for the pepper. As he tapped the shaker, slowly, deliberately, with his right index finger, a smile spread across his lips.

Oh oh, thought Osborne, *someone is up to something*.

Osborne kept a close eye on his neighbor as Ray devoted himself to smearing thimbleberry jam on his toast. Something was out of kilter, but what? Then it dawned on him: the hair!

The explosion of auburn curls guaranteed to add an inch or two to Ray's already tall frame had been tamed, as had the matching beard; it no longer served as a catchall for crumbs. *Now, isn't that interesting*, mused Osborne. While Ray liked to boast of cutting his own hair, the neat trim along the back of his neck confirmed Osborne's suspicion: this had to be a professional job.

"Are you saying that you have someone you'd like to bring?" he asked with a raise of his eyebrows. "Should I plan for six?" Osborne worked hard to keep his voice casual, but curiosity was killing him.

"Mmm," said Ray through his toast.

"Okay, then, six we are," said Osborne. "You and your friend—whoever that may be—myself, and our honorable chief of police, along with Mallory and Kent. Maybe it's Kenton. Not sure what the guy's name is."

"Sounds good to me. I'll bring fish for six," said Ray, scooping up a forkful of egg. "What time you want us there?"

"How about five or so? Let the ladies have a glass of wine. Give everyone a chance to get acquainted before we eat. That reminds me; Mallory said Kent's interested in learning to fly fish while he's up here. Darn, I forgot to ask Lew if she has the time—"

"For heaven's sake," said Ray, smearing jam on yet another piece of toast, "I can't imagine she does. August is peak tourist season. The Loon Lake police have to be busier than heck right now. Even with me behaving," he said with a smirk.

"Incidentally . . . Doc, have you noticed that ever since Jane Ericsson's crew opened their campaign headquarters, the traffic on Main Street has been horrendous? Just yesterday I must have had *seven* cars ahead of me at the light on Main and Davenport. When's the last time that happened?" Reaching for Osborne's empty plate, Ray stood up to walk over to the sink. "Anyway, it's August—the water's too warm for trout. Too warm for any fish right now."

Ray sounded glum, and Osborne sympathized. Ray's clients, the fishermen who came north from Chicago and Milwaukee, expected to get big fish, like muskies. And if they didn't hook a monster, they might never re-book. Such was the peripatetic life of a Northwoods fishing guide.

"You're right about the water being too warm for fly fishing. I'll run it by Lew this evening and see what she says. She's bringing dessert." Crumpling his napkin and tossing it onto the table, Osborne glanced over at Ray. "Mallory really wants her to meet Kent . . . Kenton . . . whatever his name is. Thinks Lew's a good judge of people."

"You're kidding," said Ray as he poured half a cup of coffee. "I would seriously, *seriously* question that, given the old coot she hangs out with." The twinkle in Ray's eye caught Osborne off guard. He blushed.

Any mention of his relationship with Loon Lake Chief of Police Lewellyn Ferris had the potential to embarrass him, perhaps because he could never be sure if she cared as much for him as he did for her.

Osborne's world had changed one night in a trout stream when "Lou," a fly fishing instructor recommended by the owner of Ralph's Sporting Goods whom he had booked sight unseen to give him a beginner lesson in casting, had turned out to be "Lew." The recommendation had been sound—Lew was indeed an expert with the fly rod—but Lew was no guy. Nor was she just a fly fisherman.

For Loon Lake Police Chief Lewellyn Ferris, that evening had proved just as valuable when she discovered her student's expertise in odontology. Teeth and dental records remained the gold standard for identifying bodies even when they have been burned beyond recognition. However, since the Loon Lake Police Department had to rely on the Wausau Crime Lab, which did not employ a full-time odontologist, it was often difficult to identify victims of suspected homicides in a timely way.

Osborne might have retired from his dental practice, but a post-grad stint in the military coupled with an enduring academic interest in dental forensics made him an expert the Loon Lake Police could use . . . and save money doing so.

Lew also saw Osborne as the solution to a more subtle in-house dilemma: the local coroner, Pecore, brother-in-law to the mayor of Loon Lake, was secure in his position thanks to family connections, but he was so habitually over-served that heaven forbid anyone in Loon Lake pass away after the cocktail hour. Too often, the cause of death certification had to wait until Pecore registered 0.04 on the Breathalyzer. But not if Chief Ferris deputized Osborne to step in as "acting coroner." Time saved. Money saved. Stress relieved.

To Osborne's delight, a friendship sparked with an unconventional exchange—lessons in a trout stream traded for assistance with the forensics of death—had evolved to become a part of his life that he treasured. Over time, the fishing had led to morning coffees shared daily, evening meals together several times a week, and to frequent cozy nights at his place or hers. It hadn't taken long for Osborne to find himself so happy around Lew that when she left a room, he was lonely.

Sipping his coffee, Ray asked, "How serious is this with Mallory? Like, is she thinking Husband Number Two?"

"All I know is Mallory seems pretty interested in the guy. They've been dating for almost six months. She's anxious for me to meet him. You, too." Osborne pulled the bowl of raspberries toward him. He popped two into his mouth. "Funny she wants our opinions. You and I aren't exactly experts when it comes to relationships, are we?"

"No, but we're good with guys, Doc. The McDonald's coffee crew hasn't kicked you out yet."

"Or you."

"And we got our pals in AA. They still let us in the door with the coffee pot on it. We have to be doing something right."

"Not sure I equate not drinking with making friends." Osborne always enjoyed these rallies with Ray. They might be silly, but the younger man was one of the few people who knew his secrets and still liked him.

"And you're sure I can bring a . . . date?"

"Of course, but I didn't know you were seeing anyone. Who's the lucky lady?"

"Girl. She's a youngster—only twenty-five. Consider her . . . a surprise," said Ray with a grin as he chomped on a final piece of bacon. Osborne was finding the grins tedious to say the least. He knew without asking that he'd have to wait until dinner to find out what was behind all this goofiness.

"Half a cup, Doc?" asked Ray, raising the coffee pot in his right hand. "Yep, this rain just may cool the water and make for some okay fishing this afternoon. If I don't catch enough,

I got two good-sized walleye in the freezer. Four, maybe five pounders."

"If you catch enough *without* the ones in the freezer, you'll be over your limit."

"True. You think the warden wants to be on water in this rain? Forecast to get heavier late this afternoon."

"Ray . . . don't do anything foolish. I'll have plenty of potato salad, cheese curds, fresh bread from the Loon Lake Market, and one of Lew's berry pies. You bring what fish you can without getting arrested, and we'll all be grateful."

Osborne *was* grateful. He could think of nothing more delicious than Ray Pradt's fresh walleye sautéed in butter. "What else is on your agenda today?"

"Got to get my hat repaired," said Ray, pointing with his fork toward the couch in the living room where a stuffed trout sat in an open FedEx box. Under the trout, whose head and tail protruded over the wearer's ears, was a well-worn leather cap with flaps that Ray wore down loose over his ears in the winter and tucked up in the summer. Across its breast, the fish wore a jeweled necklace, an antique wood-and-metal fishing lure that Ray kept polished to a high gleam.

"What's wrong with the hat?" asked Osborne.

"It's worn right through where the trout is attached. Very wobbly, see?" Ray got up from the table, plucked the hat from the box, and set it on his head. The trout drooped over one ear as its tail stuck straight up over Ray's head.

"Ouch, I see," said Osborne with a chuckle. "Ray, has it occurred to you that, at the age of thirty-two, it may be time to stop wearing a fish on your head?" Trying to repress a laugh, he snorted.

"Doc," said Ray, looking hurt. "For heaven's sake, it's my trademark, my emblem, my logo. When clients see this hat coming, all they can think is: *Excitement, Romance, and Live Bait: Fishing with Ray.* Doc, the hat is *me.*"

Osborne was sorry he'd been so blunt. "Okay, you're right. But it looks to me like the cap needs new leather at the very least. Maybe you should start over with a new cap and have someone anchor the fish on that?"

"Nope. I know just the expert who can fix it," said Ray. "She can fix anything. Hell, she makes those vinyl roofs with windows that they use on cabin cruisers. Leather repair? Piece of cake for old Kaye."

"You don't mean Kaye Lund? She butchers my deer every season. I didn't know she could sew."

Ray checked his watch. "Oh boy, I'm due at her place right now. I haven't been able to reach her on the phone, but I left a voicemail saying I'd stop by this morning. She works part-time as a greeter at Walmart; I'd like to catch her before she leaves for her shift."

"Do you think she could fix my shot bag?" asked Osborne. "Mike got hold of it last winter and chewed off the leather reinforcement where the strap attaches."

"I'm sure Kaye can handle that. Why don't you come along?"

As they stepped outside the trailer, Ray waved in the direction of his pickup. "I'll drive, Doc. Climb in."

"Thanks, but not this morning," said Osborne, clamping his khaki fishing hat on his head and adjusting the brim to keep the rain out of his eyes. "I'll get my car. Meet you up on the road and follow you over to Kaye's. Have to run by the grocery store later." With a wave, he hurried up the dirt drive to a gap between the pines where he could cut over onto his own property. The grocery store might not happen that morning, but it was a good excuse. Osborne knew better than to chance disaster riding with Ray. The passenger side door on the old blue pickup was jammed shut, which left you with two options: haul your-self through the window, or climb over the gearshift from the driver's seat. Osborne preferred holding on to what remained of his manhood, even if it cost him extra gas.

Chapter Three

Sheets of rain slammed the windshield of Osborne's Subaru. Twice he had to slow to a near stop in order to see the road. *Brother, what a day.* He'd better tell Ray to forget the walleyes. On the other hand, Ray Pradt was one of the few men he knew who *preferred* fishing in the rain: wind, rain, and ice fishing were his drugs of choice. Go figure.

Osborne felt his shoulders tense as he hovered over the steering wheel, peering through the downpour in hopes he could recognize the rock pillars guarding the entrance to the Ericsson estate. Just when he thought he had missed the driveway, he spotted Ray's taillights and turned left to follow the pickup. Though it had been years since he had driven Rolf Ericsson Drive, he remembered that final evening too well: it had been one of the interminable dinner parties that Mary Lee had loved—and he hated. The senior Ericssons were still alive at the time, and had invited fifty of their closest friends to celebrate Eve Ericsson's sixty-fifth birthday. Both Senator Ericsson and Eve have been dead a good decade or more, now. Even Mary Lee has been gone nearly three years.

While he never would have wished his late wife dead, her untimely departure from this world had allowed more sunshine into his life than he ever expected, including *no more dinner parties.* At least, not those formal, alcohol-infused events studded with the brittle preening of people he had no need to know. The blacktopped road wound down and down through an old-growth forest so ancient and with a canopy of branches so dense that not a single green plant, not even a fern, marred the rust-brown forest floor. Hemlocks at least two hundred years old loomed overhead, their trunks black in the rain. Jagged stumps split by lightning sprang from the shadows like misshapen monsters. In his youth Osborne had avoided woods like these, convinced they were haunted.

Perhaps he had been right. Land like this was a relic of another time and place. Everyone who grew up in Loon Lake knew the history: the first generation Ericssons were lumber barons wealthy enough to be among the few able to protect their property from the clear-cutting that savaged the forests of northern Wisconsin in the 1800s.

Osborne wondered if Jane Ericsson, the fourth generation and only child of the senator and Eve, valued the old-growth timber like she should. One of the few forests of its kind in Wisconsin, it might be modest in size, but it was a priceless gift. He hoped that she had taken steps to preserve it. After all, she was in her late forties, unmarried and without children of her own. When she was gone, who would inherit these glorious woods? A developer? That would be a crime.

He slowed to a stop behind Ray, who had jumped from his truck to move a fallen branch blocking the road. Osborne waited to see if extra hands were needed, but his neighbor tossed the branch out of the way as if it were a toothpick—when you're thirty-two years old, you can do that.

Falling limbs had to be a constant hazard on the private drive. Was Jane comfortable living out here all by herself? Then he remembered their reason for being there: Kaye Lund lived out here, too. So that was good. Neither was living in isolation.

Quick to admit to being an overly protective father and grandfather, Osborne could not help but be bothered by the idea of a woman living alone down a long road in a house hidden from the sight of passing motorists. This worry he applied to one woman in particular: Lewellyn Ferris. More than once he had admonished her that she was risking danger living so far from town in a little farmhouse located a half mile from the highway, and well out of earshot of neighbors.

"You could call for help, sweetheart, but no one could ever hear you," he must have said a dozen times, partly hoping to persuade her to spend more time at his place.

"Doc," Lew would respond with a pat on his arm, "I appreciate your concern but I have a badge, a cell phone, a walkie-talkie, a twenty-gauge shotgun by my kitchen door, and a Sig Sauer nine millimeter on my hip. I got it covered." Rolf Ericsson Drive wound for half a mile—past a decaying tennis court, past the remnants of a shooting range, past a putting green that appeared to have been restored—before reaching the original lodge, which had served the senior Ericssons as their summer retreat from Lake Forest, Illinois. The main house, built with timbers harvested on the property, had been closed for years, its river rock chimney crumbling, the slate roof green with moss.

The road skirted a brick walkway thick with weeds before ending in a circular drive fronting a wide white stucco structure adorned with an orange-red metal roof. The construction was so recent that no landscaping had been done. Wooden planks, laid over dirt, led up to a makeshift set of stairs that ended in front of a massive wooden door, intricately carved and as red as the roof. The place was humongous.

Osborne was mystified. Was this a home? Or a country club?

Ray had not stopped but turned onto a gravel road leading to the rear of the new building, where there was a four-car attached garage. A late-model black Jeep was parked in the drive near a rear entrance to the house.

Still Ray did not stop, but continued on the gravel road as it wound back to end at the old caretaker cottage for the Ericsson estate. The wood-frame two-story house was in need of a paint job, and had been for years. Faded blue shingles set off slivers of dark green trim around the windows. A cement stoop at the front door appeared to have been green in another century.

On the far side of the house was parked a beige Ford Taurus, its exterior pocked with rust over the wheel wells. Just beyond the sedan was a barbed wire fence surrounding a vegetable garden, well kept and fruitful, with tomatoes hanging heavy over triangular wooden cage supports.

After parking his truck behind the sedan, Ray jumped out and ran back toward Osborne who had pulled up behind him. Holding a dark green camouflage rain poncho over his head, he motioned for Osborne to roll down his window.

"Holy cow," said Osborne, baring his face to a spray of rain, "that's one heck of a roof on that house back there." He jerked a thumb at the stucco structure. "Haven't seen one of those before. That Jane Ericsson's new home, or is she turning the property into a golf club?"

"Not exactly Northwoods, if you ask me," said Ray with a shake of his head. "But that's her house all right. I hear it's amazing inside. Windows facing the lake are twenty feet high, and those suckers curve 'round so she's got a 180-degree view without a seam. Heard that from a buddy who worked on the construction crew."

"Okay for me to park right here?" asked Osborne. "If that's Kaye's car—"

"Yep, she's home."

As they ran for the house, Ray sheltered his hat beneath the poncho. Before they could knock the front door opened, and a large-knuckled, weathered hand beckoned them inside.

"Come in, come in, Ray Pradt, you rascal. And Dr. Osborne? What on earth brings you two out here on such a lousy day?"

Kaye Lund was a legend in Loon Lake. The only child of a young couple who owned a small potato farm east of Rhinelander, she was four years old when her father said he was going to the grocery store for cigarettes one night and never came home. Unable to manage the farm on her own, Kaye's mother moved them into Loon Lake and cleaned houses for a living before settling in as the housekeeper for the Ericssons. She died of cancer when Kaye was in her twenties.

Kaye was too pugnacious to attract men, much less a husband. An aggressive hockey player with a hot temper in her teens, in her twenties she nursed a reputation as a heavy drinker who could be downright frightening when over-served—but she redeemed the bad behavior with hard work.

Because she was strong enough to maneuver massive cylinders of paper, Kaye Lund was one of few women ever employed on the floor of the local paper mill. She liked to brag that at summer's end, she could pull a wooden dock in from a lake all by herself, a job known to require at least two men.

After her mother's death, she gave up the mill job to become both caretaker and housekeeper for the Ericssons' big house and the lake property: she settled down.

Too late. Wind, sun, alcohol, and cigarettes—not in that order—had done their damage. While Osborne knew from his patient records that Kaye was only fifty-three, she looked seventy. The skin around her eyes was wrinkled, jowls swung from her cheeks, and she had the torso of a black bear. More than once, on entering the Loon Lake Market behind a slow-moving burly lumberjack in stained Carhartt overalls, Osborne had been taken aback to find he was following Kaye Lund.

He had become familiar with Kaye and her history during the few years that she had attended the same sessions he did—the meetings in the room behind the door with the coffee pot on the front. She eventually stopped coming, but he and Ray would still call once in a while to see if she needed a ride. "Conquered that demon so far, fellas," she would say and decline.

But even as arthritis cramped her spine and shortened her gait, her eyes remained shrewd, her smile quick and wide, show-casing front teeth with just a smidgen of nicotine and caffeine stain. Contrary to expectations, given her sketchy lifestyle, Kaye's mouth was one of the healthiest Osborne had treated: a good bite, no cavities, no gum issues.

Because she knew she was born lucky when it came to her teeth, Kaye had never failed to show up for regular cleanings. And every time, as she gazed into the mirror after Osborne had finished, she would say, "You know, Dr. Osborne, I may not be pretty but I got a helluva smile." She did indeed. As Osborne got to know her over the years, he considered that generous grin a testament to a wild but kind heart.

Because he was never hesitant to barter with patients who did not have the money to pay for his services, he and Kaye had made a deal early on: she would butcher his deer in return for six-month cleanings and checkups, an arrangement she had insisted on even after his retirement. Kaye took pride in the butchering, which was a tough job few women tackled, much less women her age.

"Honest to Pete, Kaye, don't you check your phone messages?" asked Ray, shaking the rain from his poncho as he stepped through the doorway.

"I got a new phone with a new number. Lost my other one in the lake when I was out jigging for panfish couple weeks ago. Have to jig these days, y'know, the shoulder is so bad. Why, what's up, kid?"

Glancing back over his shoulder, Ray grimaced at Osborne. "Kaye has been calling me 'kid' since I was five years old."

Holding his hat out to her, he said, "Kaye, it's what's *down* is the problem. See where this is worn? And how my beautiful fish slumps over to one side?"

Kaye took the hat from Ray and gently flipped the stuffed trout back and forth. Osborne heard the fabric rip. "Holy cow, this hat is in awful shape," said Kaye. "Could be this fish deserves to be released?" She poked her hand through a hole that had appeared behind the fish and waved her fingers.

Ray blanched. "A disaster, huh?"

"No," said Kaye, "just a fish with a hat problem. What do you think, Dr. Osborne? Should we truss this sucker up with dental floss?"

It was a silly tease, but it was clear Kaye enjoyed toying with Ray. "I assume you're planning to pay me in bluegills?" She winked at Osborne.

"Cold, hard cash," said Ray. "Up front if you want. But," and he flinched as he spoke, "I'm afraid I really need it fixed right away—if that's possible." Ray held his breath. Worry had trumped his habit of stretching out sentences. Or maybe he didn't want to risk annoying a person with control over one of his most precious possessions.

Kaye pointed toward a yellow Formica-topped table that filled the galley kitchen behind her. "You boys sit down there while I take a good look at this critter."

Ray's hat in hand, she hobbled toward a rocking chair in the corner across from the kitchen. Sitting down, she reached for a pair of glasses on the table beside her. With deft fingers, she pushed and pulled at threads holding the crown of the well-worn cap in place.

Ray pulled out a chair, sat down and exhaled.

Before taking a chair at the table in the small kitchen, Osborne leaned forward to study a group of framed photographs hanging on the wall. On the left were two black-and-white photos of a woman that he guessed were taken sometime during the 1950s.

"Kaye, is this your mother?" asked Osborne.

Kaye looked up from where she was working on the hat. "If you mean the pictures near the fridge, yes. I had those framed years ago. I never looked much like my mom; guess I took after the old man. You know, short and fat." She barked a laugh.

"Kaye," said Ray, "that's not true. My dad told me you were really something as a girl."

"Your dad, huh. Well, maybe. We all have our window, don't we?" Kaye yanked at a loose thread. "I don't know who sewed this sucker for you but I swear they used fishing line—one-hundred-pound test, dammit." She gave the cap a shake, then said, "Jeez Louise, trying to get a hold on this without crushing the fish ain't easy."

She looked over at Ray, a crafty expression on her face. "Speaking of windows, kid, you had yours, did you not?" She winked. It wasn't a question, and Osborne had the odd sense that someone new had just entered the room.

"What are you two talking about?" he asked. He doubted they were discussing anything he didn't already know about Ray: the file of misdemeanors in Lew's office relating to the inhalation (if not growing) of a certain controlled substance, the incidents of poaching on private water, the violations of bag limits on walleyes ...

A warning glance from his friend caught him off-guard. "What?" asked Osborne, confused. As Ray's face fell, Osborne realized he should have kept his mouth shut.

"You tell him, or I will," said Kaye.

A sheepish expression on his face, Ray said in a low voice, "Oh, just something that happened ... when I was a kid ..."

"Six-t-e-e-n," said Kaye, her voice ringing across the small room. "You were sixteen. Now, be honest, Ray." Osborne glanced from Ray to Kaye, and back to Ray. A belligerence had crept into the woman's voice. So much so that he wondered if she had started drinking again.

"Yeah ... I was sixteen, and, um ..."

The rocker creaked. "Stop mumbling."

"Umm ... Jane was here for a stretch that one summer. It was right after ..." Ray choked on his words. A minute went by, but he remained silent.

Osborne gave him a funny look. He couldn't remember the last time Ray had been tongue-tied.

"It was right after her divorce. Then what happened?" said Kaye. "The rest of the story, or I won't fix your hat."

"*You* and Jane Ericsson got together?" asked Osborne. "Ray, the woman must have been—"

"Thirty," said Kaye. "She was thirty, wasn't she, Ray?" Kaye spoke with a smirk on her face. Osborne felt a growing sense of discomfort. The Kaye Lund badgering his friend—a man he knew to be guilty of grievous mistakes, but never one of unkindness—was not the Kaye Lund he knew and liked.

Ray's face had turned so red, Osborne felt sorry for him. "Listen, you two," said Osborne, "my granddaughters have a saying:

'TMI.' It means 'too much information.' I have heard enough, okay?"

Rocking her chair with a vengeance, Kaye chortled. Osborne turned his attention back to the photos on the wall, determined to ignore any new details that might be offered. After a minute had passed with no further commentary from the rocking chair, Ray gave a low sigh of relief. Of the two black-and-white photos on the left, the top one must have been a high school graduation portrait. The girl in the picture had a shy smile and straight dark hair cut in bangs across her forehead. She wore a dark sweater and a single strand of pearls. The second picture, just below, was of the same woman but a few years older. This time the camera showed her standing in heels and a dark-colored dress against a lilac bush in full bloom. In her arms she held a baby wearing a white christening gown that flowed down to the mother's knees. Osborne didn't have to ask who the baby was.

Over the center of Kaye's kitchen table hung three enlarged photos—these in full color—that had been taken in the summertime. In the first picture, Kaye appeared to be about ten years old, and the other youngster maybe four or five. The photographer had captured the girls in midair, leaping side by side over a bright red wheelbarrow, eyes shining with delight.

Next was a picture of the same two girls in swimsuits, older now, diving simultaneously from a raft into the brilliant blue of a lake. The third photo showed them standing on a dock, still in their swimsuits, with arms entwined as they smiled for the camera. Osborne guessed Kaye to be around fourteen in the latter two photos, while the younger girl, though taller, had the string-bean awkwardness of an eight-year-old.

"I didn't know you had a sister, Kaye," said Osborne as he studied the pictures.

"I don't. That's JT, back in our sister days."

"JT?" asked Osborne.

"Janie, you know, Jane Ericsson. Growing up, we called her JT—short for Jane Therese, which is what her mother insisted on calling her. Funny you ask if I had a sister. Until her folks sent her away to school, I felt like she *was* my little sis.

"But things change, always change, can't beat change. Umm . . ." With a yank of her teeth, Kaye pulled a thread that released the trout from its anchor on top of the leather cap. Setting the fish in her lap and letting the cap dangle from her right hand, Kaye leaned back in the rocker as she spoke. "My very first job was babysitting JT. I couldn't have been more than ten, and she was four—a smart aleck little kid." She grinned at the memory.

"Brother, did we have a good time in those days. I taught JT where to catch the biggest crappies, how to shoot a .22, how to catch fireflies. My mother was close by if we needed anything, but mostly we had all day to ourselves.

"Yep, I took care of JT every summer till she turned twelve. That picture of us diving—that was the year we named ourselves 'the summer sisters.'" Osborne heard sadness in her voice.

"You two are still close, aren't you?" asked Ray. "Taking care of the property the way you do, getting everything in that big new house into tip-top shape when she comes to stay? That must be kind of fun. I imagine you're getting quite a kick out of her running for her old man's seat in the Senate."

The rocker stopped. "She fired me. Six weeks ago. Out of nowhere. JT stopped talking to me, told me to stay away from the house, keep my nose clean. Hired Choppy Pulaski to take over upkeep on the property. Choppy, of all people." Kaye snorted. "Can't keep his pickup running, much less a chainsaw. But I heard what she said. Haven't seen her, spoken to her since.

"When it comes to that campaign she's running, all I can say is she's got some beauts workin' for her. Real beauts. But, hey it was bound to happen. You boys know what they say . . ."

Ray was quiet. Osborne hesitated to breathe. He watched as Kaye pushed herself up from the rocking chair. She staggered slightly as she started to cross the living room. Setting her feet wide apart, she paused to get her balance. Lowering her big head to stare at Osborne and Ray, she repeated her words: "You know what they say—the goddamn apple don't fall far from the tree. Dr. Osborne, you, me, and Ray here, we know: the woman's a drunk. Just you watch—she'll screw up."

At the look on Ray's face, she raised a hand, "Don't argue with me, kid. Takes one to know one."

The fierceness in Kaye's demeanor sapped the room of the camaraderie that had warmed it.

A heavy drinker, Jane's father had been forced out of office after leaving the scene of a drunk driving accident in which a family of five was killed. He was spared a prison sentence only because of his influence and money, which bought an expensive but effective legal defense out of Madison.

The senator was also an inveterate womanizer. One of Osborne's coffee buddies, Ike French, had captured the senator's habit succinctly as they commiserated over steaming cups of coffee at McDonald's one winter morning. It was Ike who said (and had been quoted so often since that he worried it would be etched on his headstone): "Our esteemed leader has so many notches in his belt it's amazing the damn thing can hold his pants up."

The remark got a rueful laugh, as more than one of the men sitting around the table that morning had wives, sisters, daughters, or nieces who'd been targets. And too often targets successfully seduced in spite of warnings. The late senator may have been a sinner, but a sinner who radiated charm.

One day the charm ran out. Late on a cold November Saturday, after a University of Wisconsin football game (Wisconsin lost), his body was found in the gutter of a back street in Madison. It was rumored he had been with a prostitute when something went wrong. Cause of death was a stroke that had occurred approximately three hours before the body was found.

On the plus side, as a leader in legislation benefitting the timber industry, potato farmers, and cranberry growers, Senator Rolf Ericsson III had represented Wisconsin's economic interests well for over twenty years. And he contributed to the local Episcopalian church, which had redeemed him in the hearts of some Loon Lake residents.

"I'm only living in this house because the senator deeded the house and the land it sits on to my mother after he bought our farm," said Kaye with a growl. "No sirree, the candidate doesn't want to see me, and I do not wish to discuss this further."

"Well," said Ray, "I guess that means Doc and I don't get a tour of the mansion, right?"

Kaye glared, then melted. "Sorry, boys, not your fault you hit the wrong button. Get up and follow me to my workroom. Let's see what we can do about this hat." She opened a door off the living room that led to garage-like space with a low ceiling, concrete floor, and double doors opening off the far end. The room was divided into two areas. One side held an old ping-pong table with an industrial-type sewing machine bolted down at one end. On the other side of the room was another long table, which was supported by sawhorses. Along the wall behind that table were hung tools that included a butcher handsaw, a rack of black-handled knives, and a white metal cabinet. A meat hook was suspended from an overhead beam, and two rolls of white butcher paper leaned against the cabinet. Near the double doors at the far end of the room was a large upright freezer.

The double doors were familiar. Osborne would hang the buck or doe that he had shot from the large hooks on the waiting wooden rack outside those doors, and knock to let Kaye know it was there. They had an annual ritual: the door would open and Kaye, clad in a bloody apron, would wave, saying, "I'll put your tag on it, Dr. Osborne. Never fear."

Days later a box of venison ground with pork, cut into chops or roasts, all wrapped in white butcher paper, would appear at his back door, each package with its contents marked and dated. Kaye was such an expert at dressing a deer, not to mention making sure you got *your* deer back, that hunters called months before the season opened to be sure they were on her list.

"Welcome to my domain," said Kaye, her good humor restored, as she shuffled toward the table with the sewing machine. She pointed at the table. "Nice, isn't it? I found it at a flea market a few years ago and Butch Stevens fixed it up for me. Makes it so easy to cut materials."

Behind the sewing table was open shelving filled with rolls of fabric. Osborne could see plastic and vinyl, and materials likely used for upholstery. Thinking of his chewed shot bag, he scanned the shelves for leather but didn't see any.

"Now, Ray, I don't have to be at work until noon today, so I'll get a start on your hat. I'm going to replace the leather across the top and re-anchor your buddy here. Have it for you first thing Monday morning."

"Wow, that fast?"

"That fast. You're lucky; I have leather just the color we need. Made some chaps for a Harley guy's girlfriend and had plenty leftover."

"Say, Kaye," said Osborne, "my dog chewed a hole in my best shot bag right where the leather is reinforced—"

"Bring it on, Dr. O." She smiled up at him. "That's an easy fix."

"Great, I'll drop it off later this week. Ray, you ready to get going?" Osborne checked his watch. "I have to get to the grocery store before noon."

"Out of here, you two. I got work to do," said Kaye, herding them back into the house. Just as Osborne reached to open the front door, Ray stopped and turned. A second later, the trill of a spring robin filled the room. Kaye laughed.

"Wait, you two," she said. "Open the door and listen."

Osborne did as she said, and the two men stepped onto the front stoop. Kaye pushed past them, raised both hands to her face, and let loose with a strange cry. Osborne recognized the howl of a wolf. The hair stood up on the back of his neck. The first time he had ever heard that sound was when he had been hunting grouse alone on a deserted logging lane east of Loon Lake. The wolf had seen him first and was waiting, ears up, lips curled back, teeth bared, staring. Osborne had fired his shotgun into the air, but the animal hadn't flinched. It just stared.

Later he would learn the significance of that stare—it was a challenge—but even not knowing that, it was enough for Osborne. He would never forget how fast he had run for his car. As he had fumbled his key in the lock, he heard the howl. A low-pitched long, long howl: a cry for the pack. So piercing, so loud, so unrelenting was Kaye's howl that it had to carry for miles. Osborne half expected a wolf pack to come roaring at them from the woods behind the old house.

"My God, Kaye," said Ray when she dropped her hands. "What on earth was that?"

"My war cry."

As they crossed the front yard toward their vehicles, Osborne stopped Ray to ask in a low tone, "Do you think she's been drinking?"

Ray shrugged his shoulders and said, "One thing's for sure: I wouldn't want to be Jane Ericsson right now."

Osborne backed out, then turned to lead the way down the long drive to the county road, through the steady downpour of rain. As he drove he thought about Kaye's behavior. *What was she thinking? Why embarrass Ray like that? She adores the guy, for heaven's sake.*

Then it dawned on him: The news media would go berserk with a story that Wisconsin's leading candidate for the Senate had seduced a teenager when she was a young divorcée twice his age. That could be a death sentence for Jane Ericsson's political career. Yes indeed, a death sentence.

Well, Ray certainly wasn't likely to mention it to anyone. Was Kaye thinking that Osborne would? Or was this an early warning to Ray that she would be telling others?

As he passed the black Jeep parked in the rear driveway of the big house, Osborne felt a wave of sorrow for a sisterhood broken. *After all these years.* He shook his head and drove on.

Chapter Four

By three o'clock that Saturday afternoon, eight inches of rain had fallen in less than twenty-four hours. And that was on ground already saturated from two weeks of rain or drizzle, off and on.

While the moody, wet skies might cool the August lakes and keep fishermen happy, their families grew frustrated. Loon Lake had only one movie theatre and a day's worth of shops selling ice cream and souvenirs. Rain dampens tourism.

In the offices of the Loon Lake Water Utility, tourism was the least of their worries. The unexpected heavy rainfall posed a serious threat to the nascent storm sewer system, which was only partially completed. Several intersections in town were completely flooded, and entire neighborhoods were discovering water rising in their basements.

But what was keeping the water utility manager, Bert Gilligan, working around the clock was the fact that some engineer had miscalculated the potential flow of storm waters from the network of streams emptying wetlands within the town limits. The result? A deep, black, fast-flowing river had replaced a half-mile of backyards. Lawns that once hosted picnics had disappeared under the churning waters. A brick doctors' office tilted sideways as the rushing water ate away at its foundation.

The Saturday morning downpour compounded the risk of flooding, and prompted Gilligan to issue a town-wide alert for Loon Lake residents to avoid the streets around the impromptu riverbed. Volunteer firemen were pulled in to keep watch, should the water crest above the culvert that was supposed to carry the runoff into the Tomorrow River. The culvert, due to be replaced, ran under sleepy little Woodland Avenue, which had morphed overnight into a bridge with no guardrails.

To emphasize the danger, Gilligan instructed the volunteer crew to park their trucks on the bank beside the river and to stay in their vehicles. "If that road gives way, if we get a flash flood—I don't want anyone getting swept into the water. *You may not survive.*" Of course, the warning had the opposite effect: a multitude of Loon Lake residents and tourists, cell phones held high, gathered on the street, in awe of the angry water.

That was the scene on Woodland Avenue at three P.M. that Saturday. So wild was the water that no one noticed two white packages, each the size of a three-pound roast, that were swept through the culvert. Hard to spot amid the tangle of brush, cans, plastic garbage bags, and other trash that was pushed along by the swirling river, the packages bobbed along en route to the Tomorrow River.

Chapter Five

Kitchen windows open to the murmur of the rain, Osborne set six bright blue placemats on the round oak table. He followed that with the sturdy white dinner plates that he bought after giving the flowered china that Mary Lee had insisted on using to Goodwill. Not even his daughters wanted china so delicate that it couldn't go in the dishwasher.

He set the silverware with care, remembering the amusement of Erin, his youngest daughter, when he had hosted his first family dinner all by himself: "Dad, forks go on the left. *Always.*"

Finishing with his favorite water glasses, the ones etched with tiny fish, he remembered the afternoon when he and Lew had stumbled on them in the window of an antique shop up north. They had stopped for a late lunch after an early morning of fly fishing and were walking back to Lew's pickup when they'd spotted them. Every time he used the glasses he recalled that day—the fly fishing, the lunch, finding the glasses, the intimacy of the evening that followed—and every time the memory made him smile.

Osborne stepped back to admire his handiwork. He was learning to let the sculptor's eye he had brought to his dental practice enhance his domestic skills. It might be a homely kitchen table he was setting but he aspired to a visual harmony as demanding as the arc of a fly line: the ultimate effect should be pleasing to the eye, whether human or trout.

Hmm. The table looked good, but something was missing. Before he could decide what was that was, he heard a swoosh of tires through water. A patter of footsteps followed, and the screen door off the mudroom slammed open.

"Down, Mike," said Osborne as his black Lab galloped through the kitchen to welcome the visitor.

"Sorry, Doc, but I am dripping all over your floor. Jeez Louise, am I soaked," said the dark-eyed, tousled-haired woman who strode into the kitchen shaking her head like a retriever surfacing from a swim in the lake. She unbuckled the belt holding her Sig Sauer 9 mm and laid it carefully on the counter before asking, "Got a towel handy?"

"Maybe," said Osborne, "but only if I get a proper greeting first."

Before he could reach for a hand towel on the rack beside the sink, she was up on her toes with a swift kiss on his lips. Delight sparked in Osborne's heart.

Though it had been three years since the night they met in a trout stream, the warmth in Lew's eyes, the caress of her voice, kept him wishing to have moments like this forever. A dangerous wish, he knew. The loss of his mother when he was six had taught him that what seemed so safe and comforting in life could vanish in an instant. But he wished it anyway.

"Table looks lovely, Doc," said Lew as she bent over to give her hair a brisk rub with the towel.

"That uniform of yours is soaked through," said Osborne, resisting the urge to unbutton the khaki shirt that was one half of her summer police uniform. Instead he minded his manners and was satisfied by relishing the sight of the wet cloth clinging to her full breasts. Observing Lewellyn Ferris, wet or dry, never ceased to have a mesmerizing effect on Osborne. It made him happier than he had ever expected to be. Though she was the least feminine of the women who had attracted him over time (starting when he was six years old and fell in love with Carolee Kaupinnen, who lived three doors away), in his eyes Lew was well proportioned for her height: stalwart, with a ruggedness he found sexy. More than once he had witnessed her physical strength when a clueless miscreant had challenged her authority as the Loon Lake Chief of Police.

While his late wife had excelled in the feminine rituals of home decorating, flower arranging, and the execution of bridge club luncheons, Lew was focused on carving time from her busy days in law enforcement to cast a trout fly, hunt for grouse, drop a walleye jig through frozen water, or take a refresher class in martial arts.

With a twinge of guilt, Osborne had to admit he preferred the woman whose small leather tote packed extra leaders and fly line—never lipstick. "Let me shower fast and I'll be right back to help," said Lew. "When does everyone get here?"

"Mallory and this new boyfriend of hers are due any moment," said Osborne. "They left Chicago six hours ago and haven't called, so I assume they've had no problems."

"Let's hope not," said Lew. "The switchboard was getting reports of serious flooding on a number of the roads around town, including a section of Highway 8. The storm sewer construction site off Woodland Avenue is a disaster waiting to happen, and a section of Forest County got ten inches last night. That's why I'm so wet. I assigned Roger to keep watch overnight with one of the crew from the water department, but I wanted him to grab something to eat first, so I took the watch this past hour. Had to keep getting out of my cruiser to flag idiots who thought they could drive through the flooded street."

With a shake of her head, Lew said, "Doc, what are some people thinking? They see rushing water—no telling how deep it is—and it doesn't register that driving through it might be dangerous? Honestly!"

"Whoa. The flooding is that bad?" asked Osborne. He began to worry that Mallory and her friend might be stalled somewhere in an area with no cell phone service.

"Let's just say this weather has ripped Loon Lake a new river, one with a current that could move a Ford 160 pickup," said Lew. "The engineers designing the storm water system did not take into account the impact this amount of rain might have on the wetlands and the water table." She grimaced. "What we have in the middle of town is an underground stream that has surfaced in full fury."

"Does that mean you have to work tonight?"

"I hope not. The sheriff's department is sending deputies over in shifts, too. All we can do is keep watch and hope the rain subsides soon—so cross your fingers that happens. Hey, I'm off to the shower."

"Go right ahead. I'm giving Mallory and her friend the guest rooms and bath downstairs. Oh, I almost forgot—Ray is bringing a date."

But Lew had disappeared into the bedroom and didn't hear him.

Chapter Six

Osborne checked his watch. It was nearly five, and he had encouraged Ray to arrive at five-thirty, which meant he might show up by six. His neighbor was famous for living on "Ray-time"—an arbitrary pattern of arrivals and departures dependent on whether or not the fish were biting, or if he happened to stumble on an attractive female in need of charm.

The good news was that when Ray did arrive it would be with the walleyes cleaned and ready for the skillet, which was on the stove, with two sticks of butter and a bowl of seasoned flour alongside.

Everything else was ready: the "homemade" potato salad from the Loon Lake Market was in the fridge, and twelve ears of fresh corn were husked and ready to be dropped into boiling water. There was more butter on the table along with salt and pepper.

Osborne surveyed his kitchen table. Something was missing—but what? As if she had heard him thinking, Lew stepped into the kitchen wrapped in a bath towel. "Doc, I forgot to bring in my peach pie. It's on the floor in front of the passenger seat—"

"I'll get it," said Osborne. Grabbing a poncho from its hook in the mudroom, he sloshed his way across the yard to the driveway and Lew's cruiser, where he found the pie safe in a plastic carrier. Being careful not to let the pie tip sideways, he tried to avoid slipping in the mud as he hurried back to the house. The rain gave no sign of letting up. Nor did his worry over Mallory. She had planned a four-day visit so she could show her sweetheart around. It would be a shame if that couldn't happen.

After setting the pie on a brass trivet in the middle of the kitchen table, Osborne stepped back, pleased with the results: Lew's peach pie was just what the table needed. Its crust was golden brown around the edges, and peach juices had left glossy bubbles between the strips of pastry woven across the top.

The screen door burst open with a bang. Mallory heaved the straps of a black duffle from one shoulder. It landed with a thump. Holding the door open, she waited as another black duffle entered, followed by a man in a dark green Filson Field Jacket— the same jacket Osborne coveted but refused to buy for himself, because it was too expensive.

Osborne hurried into the mudroom to help. "Welcome home, sweetie. Do you have more luggage in the car? Can I give you a hand?"

"No, Dad, this is it for now. Kenton brought his computer, but we can get that later." She reached up to give Osborne a hug and a kiss on his cheek, then stepped back to introduce the man standing behind her. "Dad, this is Kenton Harriman. Kenton, I'd like you to meet my father, Dr. Paul Osborne."

"Pleased to meet you, Kent," said Osborne extending his hand.

"Kenton," said the man as he shook Osborne's hand. To Osborne's surprise, the man's grip offered so little resistance that he had to make an effort not to crush his fingers. Of slight build, Kenton appeared to be no more than an inch or two taller than

Mallory. Even though he could not be more than forty years old, give or take a few years, a receding hairline with a dusting of grey on the temples gave him the appearance of someone much older. The face beneath the wide forehead was winter white, which was to be expected for someone with a desk job. Thin lips, a slender upturned nose and a narrow jaw left an impression of softness but his eyes were watchful, alert. Was that what attracted Mallory?

Thirty years of dentistry made it impossible for Osborne not to notice the artificially whitened teeth that had been overcorrected by an orthodontist lacking a sense of proportion. Immediately upon having that thought, he gave himself a mental slap: *For heaven's sake, you have barely spoken to the guy. Give him a break.*

"Oh, Kenton, just look at this beautiful table Dad set," said Mallory as she walked through the kitchen. "Peach pie? Dad, what a treat."

"Lew made it," said Osborne with pride.

Mallory knelt to greet Mike, who was demanding his usual rub behind the ears. Kenton stood behind them, watching. After assuring Mallory that he still loved her, the black Lab rushed over to nuzzle the newcomer in his favorite rude spot. Raising a knee, Kenton backed away.

"Off," said Osborne in a sharp tone, and the dog obeyed. "Sorry, Kent, Mike loves people. He goes a little overboard. Do you have a dog?"

"I don't," said Kenton in a tone that implied he had no plans to *ever* have a dog.

Strike two, thought Osborne even as he was ashamed of himself. He knew what Lew would tell him later: "Stop behaving like an overprotective father. Mallory and Erin are big girls now. Your job is to stay out of the way."

"Dad," said Mallory, giving Osborne the dim eye. "The name is *Ken-ton*." She emphasized the syllables. "And he's a city boy, so cut him some slack. Okay?"

"Kenton it is. Sorry about that," said Osborne, "Years ago when I was in boarding school one of my close friends was named Kent. Habits die hard, I'm afraid." He smiled an apology at the two of them. Sometimes Mallory was too much like her mother. She knew it, he knew it, and it was what made for distance between them. Osborne resolved to do the right thing: he would get the guy's name right if it killed him, *and* he would stop staring at his teeth. "Okay, you two, you've got the downstairs all to yourselves. Two bedrooms, a full bath and, if this rain ever stops, you can walk right out onto the patio—"

"Wi-Fi?" asked Kenton.

"Oh, I don't think so," said Mallory. "You don't have Wi-Fi, do you, Dad?"

"Funny you should ask," said Osborne, putting an arm around Mallory's shoulders. "I had it added to my cable service last month. Just for you."

"You did?" Her delight forgave him for slighting her friend's name. "Come on, Kenton, let's get our stuff downstairs. And Dad, we'll use Erin's old room with the view of the lake." Osborne got the message.

A knock on the back door and a glimpse through the window of a black umbrella bouncing toward the house signaled the arrival of the last of the dinner guests. Before he could reach the mudroom, Osborne heard the screen door slam shut.

Loud whispering was followed by the Slinky-like appearance of a pair of white cargo shorts showcasing two long brown legs in Keen sandals. Osborne recognized the legs: his neighbor's six feet, six inches had a way of unfolding in sections such that people who knew him swore that each section entered a room seconds before the next.

The shorts heralded the arrival of a candy-cane pink shirt dotted with orange shrimp. One of the arms extending from the shirt's short sleeves carried a bulging Ziploc bag that plopped into the sink, while the other held out a platter of fresh shrimp arranged with care in concentric circles surrounding a bowl of cocktail sauce.

"Got the walleyes, Doc," said Ray, pointing to the bag in the sink. "Two just over twenty-two inches each and a good three pounds—filleted and ready for the frying pan. Plenty for everyone."

"Ray, you've outdone yourself catching walleyes in this weather," said Osborne. "But what's with all the shrimp? You shouldn't have—"

"But I did," said Ray. "Check it out," he added with pride as he pointed from platter to shirt. "They match."

"I see," said Osborne, flabbergasted.

"Oh, Ray, those shrimp look wonderful," said Lew, who had entered the kitchen and was peering over Ray's shoulder. She looked fresh and relaxed in black pants cuffed at the knee and a sleeveless black top. Under the cluster of shiny black curls crowding her forehead, her cheeks gleamed a pale rose that reminded Osborne of a summer sunset.

"But, people," said Ray, raising his left hand as if to halt a parade, "await the *real* surprise." He turned back toward the mudroom. With a bow and a beckoning arm, he said, "Is it ... the tiger ... or ... the lady? Ta-d-a-a ..."

As he spoke, a tall, slim woman with a sheepish smile on her face appeared in the doorway. She was striking in white pants and a black and white striped T-shirt. Her hair was the color of honey streaked with sunlight, tucked up in a clip that left wisps framing a face of generous features: wide-set cheekbones, large, demure blue eyes, and an open, easy smile. As she entered the kitchen Osborne could see she wasn't just tall—she was almost as tall as Ray.

"Christina, I want you to meet Dr. Paul Osborne and Ms. Lewellyn Ferris, who happens to be our Loon Lake Chief of Police. Don't let her loveliness deceive you—she can take down a tight end for the Packers. Doc is the neighbor I was telling you about—"

Before Ray could say more, Mallory crowded into the kitchen, pulling Kenton behind her. "Ray Pradt, what the hell?" said Mallory, taking a step back in mock surprise. "Does that shirt glow in the dark? "Without waiting for an answer, she crossed the room to give Ray a hug and a peck on the lips.

She turned to Christina. "Hi, I'm Doc's daughter, Mallory," she said, pumping Christina's hand. With a wink at Ray, she said, "Anything you need to know about this gentleman here—you just ask."

"Whoa, okay," said the tall blonde, laughing. "I'm Christina Curran, and pleased to meet everyone." She gave a wave as she glanced around the room.

"Before we ask how on earth you met this razzbonya," said Mallory poking a finger at Ray, "I want the two of you—and Chief Ferris—to meet my good friend and colleague visiting from Chicago, Kenton Harriman." Mallory motioned for Kenton to step forward.

"Pleased to meet you," said Kenton, shaking hands around the room.

"Where you from, Kent?" asked Ray.

"Name's Kenton," said Kenton. Osborne tucked his chin down so no one could see the expression on his face.

"I'm living in Chicago," Mallory's friend continued, "but only for six months. Home base is Boston. I'm vice president and director of media relations for GSC Advisors, the parent company of the marketing firm where Mallory works. Guess I'm the only one here not from this neck of the woods."

"Not true," said Christina. "You are not the only stranger. I'm visiting from St. John in the Virgin Islands. Although my folks have a summer place in Manitowish Waters, which is an hour north of here, so maybe I do qualify as a local." She smiled and shrugged.

"Really? St. John and Manitowish Waters," said Mallory. "Now I *do* want to know how you know Ray."

"Wait, everyone, just hold on," said Osborne, arms out as if herding a pack of kindergarteners, "let's continue this conversation elsewhere. Snacks and drinks on the porch, and not another word until you've helped yourself. Ray, will you take the shrimp out there, please?"

Osborne's screened-in porch with its swing and comfortable wicker chairs was welcoming in spite of the storm-gray lake visible through the rain. Plates were soon overflowing with cheese and crackers, chips and salsa … and shrimp. Lew circled the room, helping Osborne make sure that everyone had something to drink before conversation picked up again.

"So, Christina," said Mallory as she popped a shrimp into her mouth, "tell us how you met Ray. I'm pretty sure he doesn't fish muskie in the Caribbean. Or do you?" She turned to Ray. "You never know what this guy has up his sleeve."

"I was the one who called Ray," said Christina. "My folks and I own an art gallery, Call of the Wild, up in Manitowish Waters. It's only open in the summertime. We specialize in wildlife art, and I happened to see some of Ray's photographs in the calendar that the Chamber of Commerce put out, the pictures of ice shanties that he took last year during the International Ice Fishing Contest.

"I fell in love with those, so I called Ray to see if he had any we might sell on consignment. Smart move on my part—they have *flown* out of the shop. Almost as popular as our hair extensions. Right now our inventory is so low that I could use some more." She turned to Ray who was sitting beside her on the porch swing. "I'd like to try some in our gallery down in St. John."

"And how did you end up in St. John?" asked Kenton. "That's quite a ways from Wisconsin."

"Our family business has been headquartered there for years. I work for my dad. Besides the art galleries, I mean. The galleries are sort of an indulgence. The fun stuff." She smiled and reached for a shrimp from the platter that Osborne held out in front of her.

"Really," said Mallory. "What do you do for your dad, if you don't mind my asking?"

"I kinda help out where needed. Right now I'm building a social media network to link all our companies."

"*Companies*. What kind of companies?" asked Kenton, sitting up so fast he knocked several crackers off his plate.

"Plastics are our main focus. We supply all kinds of plastic products to manufacturers worldwide. My great-grandfather started the business and today we have plants in China, Canada, and Brazil. Our communication between sites hasn't been the greatest, so that's what I'm working on."

"Your great-grandfather isn't Warren Buffet?" asked Kenton. "Just kidding."

"Heavens, no. But both my dad and my grandfather have developed products over the years that have been quite successful. In fact, Dad is interested in an idea Ray has, which is the real reason I drove down for the weekend. Ray, mind if I tell them?"

Ray nodded as he reached for a shrimp and gave it a careful dip into the sauce. "Go right ahead. I'd like to hear what everyone thinks."

Before Christina could say a word, Kenton interrupted. "If you need help planning out your social media development, our firm—"

"Kenton, hold on," said Mallory with gentle pat on his arm. "Let's hear about Ray's idea. You can talk our business later."

"Right, of course. Christina, I'll be sure to give you my card before you leave," said Kenton. He threw a dark look at Mallory.

"So Ray's idea is to use vending machines to sell worms. One of our companies makes vending machines, but that business has been hit hard lately, so we've been looking for ways to reinvent the industry. We're starting to sell prescription drugs and electronics in them, so why not live bait?"

"You mean worms and minnows?" asked Lew.

"Exactly. The machines could be installed in gas stations, convenience stores, bait shops, sporting goods retailers like Cabela's—"

"Sounds like one heck of a lot of worms to me," said Kenton. "What's *your* job going to be, Ray? Worm farmer?" He snorted.

"If you can farm mushrooms, why not worms?" asked Lew from where she was sitting next to Osborne. "I think this sounds like an interesting idea."

"It *is* an interesting idea," said Christina. "That's why Dad and myself and Ray are going to sit down next week and talk over the supply options. And who knows? Could be money in worms."

"I have a question, Ray," said Lew. "Those are trophy walleye you hooked today. What were you using? Worms or minnows?"

"Neither. Used an Insider Jighead," said Ray. "It's nifty—got an angled eye and presents upright. Been using it off and on this summer and having good luck with it. Speaking of which, Kenton, you fish walleye? Be happy to take you out on the boat tomorrow.

This rain may be a bummer for some folks, but it's keeping our lakes cool enough so the fish have been biting."

"Hell, I wouldn't know a walleye from a wallaroo," said Kenton. "I don't fish. Never have. Mallory's been twisting my arm to try fly fishing, but I keep telling her I hate the slimy things. I don't even *eat* fish. She loves sushi, which I cannot believe," said Kenton, pointing at Mallory with a shudder. "Yuck."

"You don't eat *any* fish? You never told me that." Mallory gave Kenton a perplexed look. "I know you're kind of vegan, but I've seen you eat steak."

Kenton shrugged. "That's different. When a client is willing to pay that much for dinner . . ."

"Excuse me, you two," said Osborne, "but back to Ray's vending machine for a minute. I agree with Lew, it's an interesting concept. Has anyone tried it? Seems to me the challenge will be keeping the worms cool if you have a power outage, which happens up here quite a bit in the summer."

"Now that is a good point, Dr. Osborne," said Christina. "We haven't even thought of that."

"While we're discussing Ray and his entrepreneurial ideas," said Lew, "I have a question. Ray, your shrimp are delicious. Is this a secret family-only recipe?"

"Yeah," said Christina. "Mind sharing the recipe?"

"Well . . ." said Ray, stroking his beard as if deep in thought.

"Oh, oh," said Mallory with a chuckle. "Here it comes."

Ray ignored her: "First, you buy the shrimp . . ."

"Of course. Come on now," said Christina with a laugh. "We're serious. We want to know. Right, Chief Ferris?"

Osborne noticed that as Ray teased the women, Kenton rolled his eyes, a sneer settling on his face. Ray caught the look on Kenton's face and paused. "Tell you what, Christina," he said, "I'll show you the spice blend I use for the boil when we're back at my place later. Chief, I'll make some up for you."

"Great," said Christina. She turned to Mallory. "So you live in Chicago? I love that city. What do you do there?"

Before Mallory could open her mouth, Kenton said, "She runs a small division for our firm. I work on the big stuff, like advising on the Senate race here in Wisconsin."

"I didn't know you're working on that, Mallory," said Osborne. "For Jane Ericsson, or for her opponent?"

"Mallory's not involved. I hope to be running a team advising on key media strategies—not the day-to-day stuff," said Kenton.

He stood up, cell phone in hand, and walked over to the swing where Christina and Ray were sitting. He leaned over Christina and held the phone out so she could see, but Ray had to twist to get a look. "Here's a photo from our pitch meeting yesterday. That's me at the head of the conference table, Jane Ericsson beside me, and next to her is this incompetent woman that she's hired as a campaign manager. Totally incompetent. I cannot wait till we can replace her."

Christina took a dutiful look, then leaned closer. "That the campaign manager? The one next to Jane?"

"Yes," said Kenton, "why? Do you know her?"

"I think I've seen her before. What's her name?

"Lauren Crowell."

"Crowell . . . Crowell." Christina shook her head. "Doesn't ring a bell. Funny though, I swear I've seen that woman somewhere . . . recently, too."

"Kenton," said Lew, "what makes you so negative about this Crowell woman? I've heard good things about her from my colleagues in law enforcement, and from several people on our Loon Lake city council. They say she's smart and tough. Well-organized.

The sheriff and I had to assign deputies to help with a motorcade she organized last week. We had no complaints."

"Chief Ferris," said Kenton with an exasperated sigh. "I spent six years as a reporter covering politics in Massachusetts for the *Boston Globe*. Trust me, I know a grandstander when I see one. The fact is, Jane Ericsson is a shoo-in. Not only does she have an impeccable record as a corporate attorney in one of the state's most prestigious firms, but add to that the wonderful family heritage: her father was one of Wisconsin's great leaders. *She can't lose.* Unless Lauren Crowell bungles it. The woman is pushy, noisy— downright obnoxious and likely to turn off key donors, not to mention voters."

"Ah," said Lew, "I imagine you know someone who can do her job better?"

"Me—or someone on my staff. Don't mean to be blunt, but you asked."

"In which case, assuming Jane Ericsson is elected, you and your firm would have an inside track in Washington. Is that a reasonable assumption?" asked Lew.

"Something like that." Kenton looked a little uncomfortable.

"I have a non sequitur question for Christina," said Osborne, eager to defuse the tension in the room. "Then I'll get dinner on. Christina, you mentioned hair extensions earlier. What on earth is a hair extension? Sounds like something you'd find in a beauty salon, not an art gallery."

"True," said Christina, "except the hair extensions we carry are works of art. They're about this long," she said, holding her hands twelve inches apart as she spoke. "These extensions are long, colorful feathers that women clip or bind into their hair. It's a fad that's been around for about a year now. We buy the feathers from the same farmers who produce them for the people who tie trout flies, and I have two women, artists really, who weave them into extensions. You know how one feather is called a hackle and a bunch are called a saddle?"

"I do," said Lew, interrupting. "I tie trout flies so I know all about that. And I have to tell you that the cost of buying good hackles has skyrocketed."

"Sorry. My customers are the guilty parties," said Christina. "Right now I cannot keep enough hair extensions in stock—we sell out almost daily. It is amazing how popular they are."

"A sacrilege is what it is," said Lew, keeping her voice soft to defuse the harshness of her words. "Let me explain why I say that. It isn't easy to breed roosters with feathers that are supple, long, and pliable enough to be used for trout flies. Takes more than a year for a rooster to grow those. I used to be able to buy feathers for a couple of bucks—the cheapest I saw the other day was over twenty dollars. For a rooster feather!"

"I know," said Christina with a sympathetic nod. "Our hair extensions start at a hundred and fifty dollars for browns and neutrals. The dyed ones run a couple hundred or more. Whatever the market can bear is what we charge."

"On that note, please excuse me while I get dinner on the table," said Osborne. "Kenton, did you mean that about not eating fish? I have peanut butter and eggs."

"Great," said Kenton, "a peanut butter sandwich would be just fine."

"Ray," said Osborne with a jab of his finger, "you're with me. Someone has to fry that fish."

Chapter Seven

Lew watched Kenton lean far forward in his chair as he checked to be sure that Ray and Osborne had made it to the kitchen and were out of earshot. *That's curious*, she thought. *I wonder what it is he doesn't want them to hear?*

When he appeared satisfied that he could speak in confidence, Kenton turned his attention back to the women sitting with him on the porch. "Help me out here," he said. "During our drive up from Chicago, Mallory filled me in on her family and friends here in Loon Lake. She talked about Ray and how his family was prominent—his old man was a doctor, and his mother was in the Junior League before they moved up north from Milwaukee. Right?"

Mallory, nodding as he spoke, said, "So?"

Kenton ignored her question, saying, "And she said that his brother is a hand surgeon and his sister has recently made partner in a prestigious Chicago law firm. Am I correct?"

Again Mallory nodded. Christina had relaxed back on the swing, which moved back and forth with a low swish.

"So what the hell happened to him?" Kenton's words hung in the air.

"If you're referring to Ray," said Mallory, "I think you need to realize he doesn't just fish. He's got lots going on—"

"Like his vending machine project," said Christina, sounding eager to defend her date.

"And he harvests leeches for local bait shops, which is not easy and pays well," said Mallory. "Leeches are prize bait up here. Not many people know where and how to find them. Plus you've got his photography, which is excellent. Right, Christina?" asked Mallory with a hint of desperation.

"He has a great eye," said Christina.

"Ray is always busy," said Mallory. "Even when the things are slow. Like he helps out at St. Mary's … um … the cemetery." Knowing she had just said the wrong thing, Mallory tried to swallow her words.

"You mean he digs graves," said Kenton with a cackle.

"People still pass away, you know," said Mallory in a small voice. Christina had stopped pushing the swing and sat silent, listening.

"R-i-i-ght. Plenty of job security there," said Kenton. "Can't argue that." Mallory's face reddened.

"On a serious note, Kenton," said Lew, keeping her tone brisk, "and one which you as a former investigative reporter will appreciate: Ray Pradt is the best tracker in the northern region. He's what we call 'a man who can track a snake across a rock.' The Loon Lake Police Department, our county sheriff and his deputies, game wardens—and the boys from the Wausau Crime Lab—we all rely on Ray when we need help apprehending a perpetrator, finding a missing person, or investigating an outdoor crime scene.

"Christina mentioned his 'great eye.' Well, Ray is the only man I know who can tell from the sign on a forest trail if a person or an animal has been there, and for how long. And, Kenton, by 'sign' I mean the tiniest evidence such as a broken twig or a patch of disturbed pine needles on the forest floor. Ray can read the sign and tell you if it was a human being, a deer, a bear, or some other critter that had passed that way. Now," Lew paused, "I'm not sure how that talent—and it is a talent—would translate to a desk job.

"I'm not finished," said Lew, with a wave at Kenton, who had opened his mouth to interrupt. "Twice he has saved my life—and Dr. Osborne's—in situations when he could have been wounded or killed. And these were situations where he had a choice: *he didn't have to help us.*

"Now," said Lew, dropping her voice conspiratorially as she made eye contact one by one with Mallory, Christina, and Kenton, "please, all three of you—can you keep what I'm about to tell you in confidence?"

Like kindergartners at story time, they all nodded, eyes wide.

"For his expertise as a tracker, Ray Pradt is ... *very* ... *well* ... *paid.*" Lew emphasized each word before adding, "On a state, federal, and local level." Glancing at the serious faces before her, she could see the point had registered.

"And that, Kenton," said Lew, sitting back in her chair, "is why Ray can afford to fish as much as he does. He may not be wealthy; he may not fit your standard of success. But he is doing what he loves. Ray Pradt is a happy man. And who can argue with that?"

A soft smile spread across Mallory's face. Christina's swing swished. Kenton looked flustered.

If Lew hadn't grown so irritated with Kenton Harriman's posturing, she wouldn't have hijacked the conversation. True, she might regret it later, but at the moment she enjoyed making Ray out to be a highly paid professional investigator, even if it wasn't quite true. At least he was paid; that part was true.

On the other hand, she left out a couple of ambiguous qualifications in his resume, including the one that the squeamish head of the Wausau Crime Lab would always use to challenge her when she invoiced for Ray's work after a successful investigation—the one to which her response was always the same: "So why didn't you say so *before* we put him on the case?"

At issue was the fact that Ray was effective at tracking down certain people because his own history of misdemeanors (not to mention brief stints in the county jail) had led to familiarity with a number of questionable characters. Among that crowd, he had a reputation of being "one of our own" who could be trusted. Looking for someone who does not pay taxes? Who has access to bath salts (not the type used in your Jacuzzi)? An individual who can fence a stolen smartphone within an hour? Very likely Ray Pradt will know someone who knows someone who will know right where to find the bad actor in question.

And then there was Ray's unique take on public relations: only he could commiserate, tell a couple of tasteless jokes . . . and score the tip that Lew or one of the Wausau boys might be searching for, *without anyone getting hurt.*

But Kenton didn't need to know everything. Nor Christina.

As for Mallory? Lew wasn't sure how much Doc's daughter knew, but she was smart enough to keep her mouth shut.

When the pie had been decimated and chairs pushed back from the table, Osborne exhaled in a combination of pride and relief. The fish could not have been flakier, the potato salad more satisfying, and the pie . . . well, Lew's peach pie was the highlight of the meal. With the dishes cleared and coffee cups refilled, the candles he had lit softened the faces around the table while the rain drummed a soothing monotone through the windows.

"Well done, Doc," said Ray, resting his right ankle on his left knee as he stretched both arms overhead. "That . . . was very tasty . . . if . . . I may say so myself."

"Kudos to Ray for the delicious walleye," said Lew, raising her coffee cup in a toast.

An impish look crossed Christina's face as she said, "Earlier, when we were discussing Ray's many virtues—" She paused to give Ray an affectionate jab with her elbow. "—we forgot to mention that he is an accomplished collector of fishing lures."

"Oh, right," said Mallory with a knowing chuckle. "So you've been introduced?"

"Kind of," said Christina. "Now, it so happens my father collects fishing lures, too, but his are for saltwater fish *and* they are meticulously stored in custom-made walnut boxes. Not this guy's—" She poked Ray again.

"Would you believe he hangs his lures from the ceiling over his bed? I mean—" Christina shifted in her chair to stare at Ray. "—Mister Pradt, you are never going to get lucky. What girl wants to roll over on a Red Rizzo Tail, for heaven's sake?"

"Or an Insider Jighead." Ray answered her challenge with a smile that implied he had not found dangling lures to be an impediment to his love life.

"If you don't mind, let's continue this analysis of Ray's love life another time," said Lew, getting to her feet. "Some of us have to work tomorrow, so if you'll excuse me . . ."

"Doc . . . it's been real," said Ray, pushing back from the table. "Time to head over to my place and find Christina a *safe* place to bunk. Say, Sparky," he said, looming over Kenton who was still sitting at the table, "I'm taking Christina out on the boat in the morning. Care to join us?"

The shocked expression on Kenton's face amused Osborne, but his response was even more surprising: "Umm, sure. Yeah, I'd like to do that."

Mallory gave her friend a puzzled glance, then looked up at Ray, "Me, too?"

"Mallory, you are as welcome as the flowers—the more the merrier. 'Night, all."

"Thank you very much for having me. It's been a fun evening," said Christina, shaking both Lew and Osborne's hands before following Ray out the back door.

When all the guests had left or retired downstairs, Lew and Osborne finished arranging the dishes in the dishwasher. Wiping his hands on a dishtowel, Osborne asked, "Did you notice Mallory's friend ate two pieces of pie?"

"That wasn't his only mistake," said Lew. "By the way, I like Ray's friend. She's a graceful girl."

"And Kenton?"

"He could use a little grace."

Half an hour later, curled around Lew in the warmth of his bed, moonlight streaming through the open window and catching the curves of her face as she slept, Osborne lay awake thinking back over the day: his irrational terror at the sound of Kaye Lund's howling; the long, memory-laden drive past the old Ericsson summer lodge; and the sight of that massive new house so obtrusive in the quiet woods.

Osborne's mind wandered as sleep eluded him. Golly, when *was* the last time he had seen Jane Ericsson? Was it four summers ago that she had joined the group that met behind the door with the coffee pot on the front? *She hasn't been there since. Is she still on the wagon?* And what would cause her to be so angry with Kaye, a woman she had known since childhood as almost a member of her family?

He remembered the black Jeep parked in the drive that morning, and thought of Jane holed up alone in her big house. Alone. Lonely. Loneliness was itself a seductive drug: an invitation to wallow in self-pity. He would never forget his own year in the abyss, after Mary Lee's death.

While he had never known quite how to handle his wife when she was alive, her death had left him at a loss for how to handle life alone. And so he had spent too many long night hours in his kitchen. The lights off. One six-pack after another. And when the beer was gone, the whiskey.

Give it up and try to sleep, Osborne admonished himself. Why lie awake and worry about Jane Ericsson, a woman he barely knew? The only time they had spoken at length was the summer just after he opened his practice. She was sixteen, and needed two cavities filled. Her mother had insisted he use gold. Osborne smiled at the memory: that young face and gentle smile were permanently captured in the patient records he kept safe in the old oak file drawers in his garage.

It was a pleasant thought. He slept.

Holding the rain poncho over her head, Christina dashed ahead of Ray to the front door of his house trailer. As she pushed it open, an envelope that had been slipped under the door blew across the floor. She picked it up and handed it to Ray.

Inside was a slip of paper that read:

"Ray, I need a special thread for your hat. Only person who has it is a friend in Rhinelander who does upholstery. Driving over first thing in the morning. Hat should be all set by noon. Not working tomorrow so stop by any time, Kaye. P.S. You owe me half dozen bluegills but I can live with walleye. J"

Chapter Eight

Roger Adamczyk yawned as he leaned back against the headrest of his squad car. What he wouldn't give for a pillow right now. On the other hand, he couldn't complain. This was the easiest assignment he'd had in months—the kind he had hoped for when he joined the Loon Lake Police Department three years ago after struggling too long trying to sell life insurance.

It was the benefits that had convinced him to go into law enforcement, a no-brainer. Not only could he retire at age fifty, but he figured Loon Lake must have so little crime, chances were he could spend his days emptying parking meters. Boy, was he wrong.

Since the day he was hired, Chief Ferris had had him working his butt off. This summer was the most stressful yet, as she had assigned him to lead the Fourth of July parade, search for stolen outboard motors, and do pre-dawn surveillance on a couple of jabones known to be raiding a private raspberry patch. Heck, last Tuesday he found himself wading chest-deep in Squirrel Lake, trying to lasso a rogue pontoon boat.

Worst of all, twice a week he'd been assigned to the night desk processing paperwork on the DUIs that Chief Ferris and Deputy Donovan brought in. What a nightmare that was. Over the last year, six of the fellas arrested for driving under the influence were buddies of his, including three who had bought life insurance from him. Talk about losing friends? Sheesh.

Yep, he deserved tonight: An eight-hour snooze of a watch on Woodland Avenue where the once-underground river overflowing the culvert had risen to nearly level with the road. His mission: if water overflows Woodland, don't let any numbnuts drive through. And, Jeez Louise, who would be dumb enough to do *that*?

Right away, he had made a deal with Stan Kowinski, the water utility worker assigned to the same watch. Each would sleep four hours while the other stayed awake.

Piece of cake, thought Roger. If the rain ended, he might even sleep through his own watch. With tomorrow off, he had plans to fish walleye on the Willow Flowage, so he needed a good night's sleep. This rain was good for something at least—cooling the lakes to where the fishing was better than usual for mid-August.

A rapid knocking on the passenger side window jolted him from his reverie. Stan's face was highlighted by the glow from the lantern he held in one hand as he motioned for Roger to unlock the door of his squad car. He did, and Stan jumped into the passenger seat.

"Hey, Rog, gotta tell you what I saw," said Stan, calling Adamczyk by his first name. They had known each other since first grade at St. Mary's. "Lucky thing I had my muskie net in the back of the pickup."

"Oh yeah?" asked Roger, rubbing his eyes. He blinked hard and peered at Stan as he turned up the interior light of the squad car. "Don't tell me that water's higher . . ."

"Nah. You know how all the basements around here are flooding?" asked Stan.

"Yeah, so? Nothin' we can do about it."

"That's not my point. Somebody's freezer must have come unlatched. I just caught six packages of prime venison that came floating by. Leastways, I'm betting it's venison. Could be nice chops, a tenderloin and backstrap if we're lucky. They aren't marked though. We'll have to guess. Wanna see?"

"Sure." Adamczyk heaved his body out of the squad car. Stan might be on to a real treat. Cops didn't get much time off for deer hunting and, boy, did his wife love a good venison steak.

Pulling the hood of his rain jacket over his head, Roger jogged over to Stan's truck. The rain had slowed to a drizzle, and the glow of a nearby streetlight reflected off the asphalt. No water was flowing across the street. A good sign. Sleep could be just around the corner . . .

Six packages, each wrapped in white butcher paper and banded with white tape, were piled on the floor mat on the passenger side floor of Stan's pickup. Roger leaned in for a good look as Stan held his lantern over the mound of roast-size parcels.

"Think it would be okay for us to rescue these?" asked Stan with a hopeful grin.

"Can't imagine why not," said Roger. "Given where all the water's going, it's you and me, or the Tomorrow River, right? Still frozen?" he asked, reaching as he spoke. The package he grabbed gave under pressure from his fingers. "Oh, oh, this one's thawed. What about the one you got there?"

Stan squeezed another package. "This one, too. Well, maybe they're no good, huh?"

"Oh, hell, I wouldn't say that," said Roger. "Let's check. If they smell okay, just cook 'em up in the next day or two. Don't you think?"

"Yeah. Sounds good to me. Maybe we should see what we got, huh?"

"I got better light in the squad car," said Roger. "Bring a couple over there and we'll take a look. I've got some old newspaper we can use in case the meat oozes."

Under the dome light in the Loon Lake Police squad car, each man laid a section of newspaper on their laps before using a pocketknife to slice through the tape securing the white packages. Roger had the smaller of the two, so he got his unwrapped first. He stared down.

The thing was six inches long with black specks of blood on what appeared to be a scattering of light brown hairs over white skin. He thought he saw tendons exposed on one end but he couldn't be sure. The foreleg of a fawn, maybe?

Stan never said a word after opening his. He leapt from the car, vomiting through hoarse, strange cries. Roger looked down at the contents of the package Stan had thrown off his lap onto the floor of the squad car.

"Argh," he choked, too stunned to scream as he scrambled backwards out of the vehicle.

Nestled in its crumpled white butcher paper wrapping was a human head: eyes half closed, blood oozing from the severed neck, black hair matted tight to the skull. He didn't wait to see if it was male or female. It sure as hell was not a venison roast.

Chapter Nine

"Dad, we won't let you do this. You're killing yourself." Erin shook him by the shoulders, her words torn with sobs.

"We love you, Dad. Please, don't you want to see Erin's kids grow up?" Tears were streaming down Mallory's cheeks as she echoed her younger sister's pleadings. In the distance, Osborne could hear the siren of the ambulance they had called to take him to rehab . . .

The trill of a cell phone pierced the quiet of the bedroom.

"Damn," said Lew, fumbling for her phone on the nightstand to her left. "What?" At the sound of her voice, Osborne realized with relief that he had been deep into a nightmare. Rehab was behind him. He was sober. Laughter and smiles had replaced his daughters' anguish.

Raising himself up on one elbow beside Lew, Osborne could hear the terror in the voices shouting over the phone. He watched Lew's face as she tried to make sense of what sounded like absolute chaos.

"Slow down, Roger. I can't make out what you're saying. Breathe. Who's that other person shouting? Hold on, let me call you back on the landline. I can hear better."

Leaping naked from the bed, Lew ran to the kitchen for Osborne's ancient phone mounted on the wall near the sink. He grabbed her robe from the hook on the door and chased after her, throwing it over her shoulders as she punched in Roger's number.

"What—" he started to ask, but she shook her head and raised a finger for him to stay silent. He checked the clock on the wall: 2:20 A.M. Pitch black outside. A light patter of rain on the roof.

"Okay, Roger, start over. But first tell me this: Do you need an ambulance? Has someone been hurt?" She listened. "Dead . . . no question? No, I believe you. Please stop shouting—well then, tell Stan to stop shouting. Now, Roger, listen to me: Nothing is going to change before I get there in fifteen minutes so both of you *calm down.*

"And you're in no danger from the flooding, correct?" A one-second pause while Lew rolled her eyes at Osborne.

"Now tell me again: who is this Stan person?" A brief pause. "I see. Well, please lower your voices—both of you—before you wake the entire neighborhood.

"Last thing, Roger—don't either of you talk to another person until I get there. That means stay off your walkie-talkie. No, do not call the switchboard. I don't want this on the scanner until I know more. I will handle notifying the switchboard. Understand? The last thing we need is some damn television crew messing us up.

"And, Roger, everything I said goes for Stan, too. He does not call his boss, his wife—anyone. Am I clear? Now, the two of you back away from your vehicles and please, try to calm down."

Lew quit the call, then punched in another number. She got a voicemail on the answering machine and hung up. For a second, she covered her face with both hands. Then, looking up at Osborne, she said, "I forgot. Pecore was called down to Madison for a hearing Friday that has been moved to Monday morning. A cold case from twenty years ago has been opened, and the lawyers don't like how he handled the chain of custody on critical evidence. Surprise, huh.

"Sorry about roping you into this, Doc, because it is one of the few times I could rely on Pecore—it doesn't take a brain surgeon to declare a severed head deceased."

Osborne's mouth dropped open. "Wha—?"

"Pull your clothes on ASAP, sweetheart. You're my deputy coroner on this, and it sounds like a doozy. Tell you what I know as we drive in."

"Okay." Osborne paused for one minute to scribble a note to Mallory before running back to the bedroom. Neither of them took the time to brush their teeth. Leaving the house, Osborne made sure to pick up his black bag with the instruments he would need. Thinking ahead, he hoped Ray was not too engaged with his houseguest as Lew might need photos, too.

Seconds later, as they hurried across the yard toward Lew's cruiser, Osborne was relieved to see the rain had leveled off to a light mist. "Doc, you drive. I have to reach the Wausau boys. This is one for them."

Reaching Woodland Avenue, Osborne would have pulled up behind Roger's squad car, but the police officer waved his arms in the glare of the headlights, motioning for them to pull over across the street. Before getting out of the cruiser, Lew finished leaving a message with the Wausau Crime Lab's night operator.

"Any luck?" said Osborne as she got out of the car.

"Yes, actually. The director is on vacation; they're trying to reach my buddy, Bruce Peters. Ought to hear from him shortly."

They started across the street. Through the mist, the street lamps threw enough light that it was easy to see both Roger and the water utility worker standing a good fifty feet away from their vehicles, as if the pickup and the squad car were themselves possessed.

Roger ran toward them. He was so pale that Osborne half expected him to faint. "Chief Ferris, you won't believe what's going on. I keep hoping this is some kind of prank." He pointed toward his squad car. "Okay if I stay back here while you—"

"Fine," said Lew. "Doc, will you hold this torch for me?" They walked over to the police squad car. The package that Roger opened lay where he had thrown it onto the wet grass beside the open door on the driver's side.

"You don't have to take a cadaver lab to know that this is part of a human forearm," said Osborne as he crouched over the crumpled wrappings for a closer look.

"Are you sure?" asked Lew. "I can't tell you how many people confuse bear remains with humans, Doc."

"It's the bones that confuse people, Lew. This is human, and recently severed. Within the last forty-eight hours or so, given the coloring and the blood."

"Male or female?"

"No idea. Let's see what else is here. That may help, but Wausau will be able to tell you for sure."

Next was the bundle that Stan had unwrapped. Lew took a quick look. "Careful, Doc, it's upsetting." She got to her feet and turned her face into the breeze, as if hoping to cleanse the sight from her memory. "I've seen a lot since I've been on the force but never anything like this . . ."

Osborne knelt on the wet ground beside the open door. He knew from experience that moving the butcher paper any more than was necessary might contaminate the crime scene. After pulling on a pair of nitrile gloves, he leaned into the squad car, keeping his head tilted to one side to avoid blocking the beam from the dome light above.

With a delicate touch, he parted the folds of the butcher paper. He stared. He could hear Lew breathing beside him as she gathered up the courage to take another look. He leaned back to reach into his medical bag.

Even before he pushed aside the dark tendrils covering the dead white face with one of his instruments, he had the sensation he had seen this skull, these cheekbones, this jaw before. Paul Osborne was a man who might forget names, but never a face.

Dropping his hands to his sides, Osborne sat back on his heels. "I hope you're ready for a shock," he said, keeping his voice low.

Lew put a hand on his arm. "Someone you know?"

"Jane Ericsson."

Lew said nothing for a long moment. "You're sure."

"Positive. And I can prove it. Back when she was a teenager, I filled a couple of cavities for her. The record will be in my files. If you need a first-degree relative for the official ID, you'll have to depend on Kaye Lund. Jane has no family left alive, but Kaye has known her since childhood."

"She'll have to do," said Lew.

"That worries me, Lew. Kaye is not a well person. This will be quite a shock."

"Oh great. Just what I need: give the only person who can identify the victim a heart attack. They didn't offer training on that at the police academy. We'll need to soften the news somehow."

Osborne nodded. "Want me to take care of it?"

Years of informing patients they needed thousands of dollars of dental work or they would lose their teeth had taught Osborne how to broach a difficult subject with the grace and sympathy that might help a listener cope.

"Please. If you would, Doc. Meanwhile, everything stays as is until I can get one of the Wausau boys up here.

"Roger?" Lew called out to the deputy who was leaning against her cruiser. "I want you to cordon off this entire block. As neighbors wake up, please explain that we can't have anyone walking, biking, or driving around here. This is a crime scene. I'll call Deputy Donovan and ask him to give you a hand."

She turned to Stan. "You need to call your boss—"

"Yep," said Stan, "Bert Gilligan's who I work for."

"Let him know what the situation is. I'll give you my cell number. He can call me if he has questions. And both of you," said Lew, looking hard at the deputy and the utility worker, "no one talks to the media except me. Got it? This is going to cause an uproar over the next few days, and I have to be able to depend on your silence—or you could jeopardize the case. Besides which, you two are witnesses. You wouldn't want the person behind this coming after you, would you?" Both men looked unsettled.

After Lew gave Roger more detailed instructions on how she wanted the squad car and Stan's pickup protected, she and Osborne headed back to her cruiser. As she shut the car door, her cell phone rang. She checked the screen before answering, and a wave of relief crossed her face.

"Bruce! Thank you for calling so soon. I have Doc Osborne here with me—okay if I put you on speaker?"

"Sure." The voice of the young crime lab expert who was a favorite of Lew's sounded sleepy. "I have a hunch you got something going that means I might get a little 'up north' time, maybe some . . . fishing?"

"Well, yeah," said Lew, managing a smile. "But, man oh man, I have a hell of a situation up here . . ." Talking fast, she laid out the situation.

"Sounds like a case they had in Milwaukee back in the forties," said Bruce. "At least we've got DNA these days and you know me—I love a challenge. Should be up there in less than ninety minutes. Meantime, here's what I need: Doc, you get those dental records and round up the family friend who can identify the victim. How many packages did you say have surfaced so far?"

"Six that I know of," said Lew. "I have two men watching for more."

"That doesn't account for any that may have drifted by earlier. Do you know where that underground stream empties?"

"The Tomorrow River," said Osborne, "and that flows into the Wisconsin on the south end of Loon Lake."

"Got it. I'll alert the DNR to keep an eye out. Doc, what's your estimate on time of death?"

"I can't tell," said Osborne, "but I see no signs of decomposition, if that helps."

"Whoa," said Bruce, sounding as if the reality of the macabre scene had just registered. "I'll bet you make the national news! Put pressure on our lab, too. Do you have Ray Pradt shooting the crime scene? I know you like to work with him."

"Not yet," said Lew. "It's been less than half an hour since I got to the scene. He's next on my list to call."

"Tell you what, Chief," said Bruce. "If you can keep the site pristine until I get there, I would like to bring one of our photographers with me. Gives us better control. I don't have to tell you that the minute you have a prominent person as the victim, the media and lawyers can make life difficult."

"Fine with me," said Lew, "I'm going to have my hands full as it is."

"Last thing, Chief Ferris, and you know the drill." Bruce might be sleepy but he knew the question to ask. "What are you offering to sweeten this deal?" It was a game they always played: when Lew was fortunate enough to have Bruce assigned to her case, she made sure to help him with his casting. He had taken his first fly fishing lessons from her at Osborne's urging and, since then, when he was assigned to help the Loon Lake Police, Bruce would try to take an extra day in order to get more instruction from Lew. Osborne made it a point to tag along; he always picked up pointers watching and listening as she worked with Bruce. Lew chuckled. "Bruce, how 'bout this—we're a month away from the World Classic Muskie Championship, which will be held up around Eagle River. A friend of mine has designed a special fly for the folks who want to go after the big girls with a fly rod. He calls it the Baby Smallmouth Bass Figure Eight. How 'bout I get you one of those and, when this is over, we'll spend some time in muskie water with our fly rods."

"Are you kidding? That's like an early Christmas. I am all yours, Chief." Bruce had thick black eyebrows that twitched when he was happy. Osborne thought he could hear them twitching over the phone.

"Bruce, thank you. You're on the clock starting now. I'm running Doc back to his place for his car then I'll be back here waiting for you."

It was four A.M. when Bruce arrived at the scene on Woodland Avenue, photographer in tow. It was quarter to six when

Osborne turned down Rolf Ericsson Drive on his way to pick up Kaye Lund. As his car wound through the grove of ancient hemlock, he felt a sadness so profound he wished he could turn back.

He drove past the big house. The windows were as dark as they had been the morning before, and Jane Ericsson's black Jeep was still parked in the driveway.

Chapter Ten

It was not easy explaining to Kaye why she had to identify her childhood friend from the mutilated remains resting on the floor of a squad car parked in the mud on Woodland Avenue. But Bruce refused to release any of the rescued body parts to the morgue until he had decided on the correct procedures, which would involve testing the butcher paper wrappings, analysis of the contents, and documentation of each stage of the search for more parcels.

Until he had finalized that plan and confirmed his approach with his colleagues at the Wausau Crime Lab, nothing and no one (meaning Roger and Stan) left the site near the now-vanishing river on Woodland.

It was impossible to tell how many parcels had traveled the waterway that night, but it was becoming clear that there would be no more, as the river was now less than six inches deep with no hint of the raging current that had been strong enough to carry the weighted parcels.

"I understand, Doc," said Kaye, after Osborne had described as gently as he could the events of the morning and how little the police knew so far. He was about to explain how Bruce's approach was grounded in proven forensic science when Kaye interrupted, saying, "Let's just get it over with."

And so it was that shortly after six A.M. they approached Roger's vehicle. An ambulance was parked nearby, awaiting a green light from Bruce. In an ironic twist, the low-hanging clouds of the previous three days had cleared, the rain no longer a threat. As the sun rose over neighboring rooftops, a pale rose suffused the sky: promise of a gorgeous day.

After pulling on a fresh pair of nitrile gloves, Osborne knelt in front of the open car door. "Can you see over my shoulder?" he asked Kaye.

"Yes." Her voice was soft, tense. Osborne pushed the crumpled butcher paper back for her to get a good view. She gasped. Sagging sideways, she grabbed on to the car door for support. Osborne jumped to his feet in time to catch her by the shoulders before she fell. As Kaye struggled for a breath, he pulled her toward him.

"I am so sorry, Kaye," he said. "No other way to do this."

"Don't talk, please don't talk," said Kaye, her words muffled against his shoulder as she continued to heave so hard with each breath that Osborne worried she might hyperventilate and pass out. After a few minutes, she steadied, got her footing, and pulled away from him.

Kaye turned to the door, closed now, and leaned against it with her arms crossed and her forehead resting on her arms. She shook. Her entire body shook. From deep inside her throat came a keening, a cry as wild as her wolf call: the cry of grief.

Osborne stepped away and waited until Kaye pushed back from the car and wiped at her eyes. When he felt she had pulled herself together, he forced himself to ask the necessary questions: "Am I right? Is that Jane?"

She nodded, blew her nose with a Kleenex Osborne had handed her, and managed to whisper in what voice she had left: "Yes. Oh, dear Jesus, yes. Who would do such a thing? What evil—" She choked. Again Osborne folded her into his arms.

Half an hour later, the two of them sitting in his Subaru, he handed her a clipboard with the documents that needed to be signed. She did so, identifying herself as a close family friend who had known the victim for over forty years.

On the drive back to Kaye's house, Osborne asked, "Will you please let myself or Chief Ferris know if you think you may have seen any strangers on the property recently? Any cars that you don't recognize?"

"That's not easy," said Kaye. "She had so many campaign workers coming and going, not to mention the guys doing the landscaping . . ." Her voice trailed off, and she shook her head as if that effort was futile.

After a moment's thought, she said, "You know, there has been one. A dark green VW van, kinda beat-up. I've seen it parked a little ways down the highway from the entrance to our road off and on this summer. Down near the Christmas tree farm. I just assumed it was one of those guys Irv hires to trim his trees. But late yesterday I looked out my kitchen window and saw a van sort of like the VW parked over in Jane's driveway. Didn't think too much about it, 'cause she's always getting deliveries when she's home. It was a van, but it was after dark, so I couldn't say if it was the same one."

"Be sure to let us know if you see it again, will you? I'm going to write down two numbers for you; one is my cell phone, and the other is the cell phone number for Chief Ferris."

"She won't mind?"

"Kaye, don't be silly," said Osborne, his voice stern. "We need all the help you can give us on this."

With that he reached for her hand and held it tight as he turned off the main road to head down Rolf Ericsson Drive. As they approached the new house, he saw there was a second black Jeep parked next to Jane's.

"Whose car is that?"

"That belongs to Lauren, the campaign manager. She stays at Jane's when they're in town."

"She certainly should not be in there right now. Chief Ferris wants no one in that house until she and Bruce from the crime lab are finished with their work."

"Good luck telling that broad anything," said Kaye as Osborne pulled up to the front door of the old caretaker's house. She sighed as she opened the car door. "What a morning. At least I have Ray's hat to work on."

Kaye looked so sad Osborne couldn't resist leaning forward to give her a hug. "I'm sure he'll understand if you don't, Kaye."

"Heavens, it's a good way to take my mind off things. Finish the hat, and then I guess I better start making funeral arrangements. No one else around to do it."

"Hold on, Kaye," said Osborne, putting his car in park as he reached for his phone to call Lew. "I want to give you those phone numbers, but first I need to let Chief Ferris know we've got someone in Jane's house."

"Doc, do whatever it takes," said Lew, answering his call immediately. "Get that person out of there. Are they nuts?"

"I'll take care of it," said Osborne.

Chapter Eleven

After making sure that Kaye made it into her house okay, Osborne tried to call Mallory, concerned that she and Kenton might be waiting on him to plan the day. No answer. He wasn't surprised. Likely they were still sleeping or Mallory had a reason (none of his business) to have her phone turned off. He left a voicemail.

He backed up and swung the car around to drive the short loop between the houses, then parked alongside the second Jeep. Approaching the side entrance to the house, he could see the door was ajar. Through the screen a voice could be heard talking so loudly that he assumed the person must be on a phone call with a bad connection—either that, or she was talking to someone hard of hearing.

He paused outside the door, eyes on the ground as he listened to a voice that was low and husky, more masculine than female. "I can't imagine where she is," said the voice with more than a trace of irritation. "The car is here but no sign of Jane . . . yes, her purse is right here on the counter—" If Kaye hadn't said that the second Jeep belonged to a woman, he would have assumed he was listening to a man.

Before he could raise his hand to knock, the figure of a woman appeared at the top of the short staircase just inside the door. She was still holding the phone to her ear as she waved at him saying, "Call you back—got someone here.

"Doctor Osborne, please come in." The woman bounded down the stairs toward him. "I recognize you from your photo, and I know you live nearby. Did Erin ask you to stop in?" She spoke fast and with such enthusiasm that Osborne found it difficult to get a word in edgewise.

Tall, wide-shouldered, and slender, the woman was dressed all in black. She had straight black hair tucked tight behind her ears and a precisely cut fringe of bangs across her wide forehead. The blackness of her hair against a pale complexion, lively black eyes, and bright red lips reminded Osborne of a childhood toy of Mallory's, a Japanese storybook doll elegant in a black and white kimono, its geisha face chalk white and painted. He was thinking of the doll as she thrust out a hand that grabbed his with a hearty shake.

"Lauren Crowell, Jane Ericsson's campaign manager, and your daughter Erin and I were just talking about you yesterday morning. Ha, ha." Her words ran into the brittle laugh without a breath. Before Osborne could jump in with his news, she was talking again: "Erin has agreed to manage Jane's campaign office here and we're hoping you might host an event for some of the professional people we want to encourage to donate—"

"Miss Crowell, please," said Osborne, desperate to halt the rush of words, "I am so sorry but I'm here to deliver some disturbing news—"

"Nope," she said, pulling her hand away and holding it up as though stopping traffic, "Lauren. Call me Lauren. None of that

'Miss Crowell' baloney. Come on in, please." She held the screen door open for him.

Before he could answer, she was back up the stairs two at a time, saying, "And, Dr. Osborne, not to worry, it's okay. I already heard—the paper mill is refusing to let Jane speak to their employees. I told Erin no big deal. Screw 'em. That's something we can work around."

He followed, trusting she had to take a breath sometime. *One thing for sure*, thought Osborne, *this woman's determination is impressive*. She might remind him of a doll, but she certainly filled the room. He sensed a toughness that would make her very good at her job—not unlike the edge that drew him to Lewellyn Ferris.

"Lauren," said Osborne, raising his voice as he walked into a large, open kitchen filled with sunlight. He went for the tone he'd perfected with six-year-olds who would not open their mouths. "Stop right where you are and listen to me: *Jane Ericsson won't be speaking with anyone*."

Lauren stared at him. She backed against the kitchen counter, bracing herself with the palms of both hands. "Car accident." She hit the words so hard Osborne knew she had been expecting such news. "Did she kill anyone? I told her the drinking was out of control." Lauren set her jaw. "Where is she? What jail? What's the bond? Any chance I can keep this out of the papers?"

"No car accident. She's dead. She's been murdered."

Lauren stared at him. "I don't believe this." She raised her right hand to her forehead then dropped it. "I don't believe this," she said again.

The kitchen area in which they were standing opened directly into a high-ceilinged living room. Across the room was a wall of floor-to-ceiling windows, which ran the length of the room and overlooked Cranberry Lake. On another day, it was a view

Osborne would pause to appreciate. But at the moment, all he wanted was for the stunned woman in front of him to sit down and pull herself together.

In the middle of the kitchen was an island with six high-backed cushioned stools on three sides. Taking her by the elbow, Osborne guided Lauren onto one of the stools. He pulled a notebook from his back pocket and sat down beside her.

"Here's what we know so far," he said, and gave her the details. As he spoke, Lauren's eyes never left his face. When he had finished, she continued to stare at him.

"You're saying . . . you are sure that . . . that was, I mean, *is* Jane?"

"We know that for a fact."

She took a deep breath, straightened her shoulders, sat tall in the stool and closed her eyes. "Give me a minute for this to sink in?" She spoke with her eyes closed.

"Of course."

Lauren sat still for a long moment, then opened her eyes to look at Osborne. No tears. "I feel so . . . flat," she said. "Just flat. And, like, wow, has my life just changed."

Osborne resisted the urge to say: "*Your* life? How about Jane Ericsson's?"

But he didn't say it. Instead, he said, "I'm very sorry but I need to help you leave this house. We can't have anyone in here until after the police and the crime lab have completed their inspection of the property, in case Jane was abducted from here. There could be evidence that will help us find the person who killed her."

"I'll move down to the boathouse—"

"No, we need you off the property, and by that I mean the house, the buildings near the water, and the grounds around the buildings. Chief Ferris and the forensic team from the Wausau Crime Lab will be here any moment."

"You're *sure* the . . . what they found is Jane?" asked Lauren as she let herself down from the stool.

"Yes. Kaye Lund, her old friend who lives next door," Osborne gestured in the direction of Kaye's house as she spoke, "she identified the remains for me. Plus I have early dental records, which will be helpful—"

"You believed that old frog?" Something mean flashed across Lauren's face. The sunlight streaming in the living room windows caught flecks of yellow in the irises of her dark eyes. Lauren Crowell might have the face of a seductress, but she had the eyes of a wolf.

"Kaye and Jane grew up together—" Osborne started to say, when his cell phone rang. "Excuse me, it's Chief Ferris."

"I'll get my things together. "Lauren started to walk away.

"Wait," said Osborne, holding the phone away from his ear as he grabbed her arm. "I need to come with you to be sure we enter and leave the rooms on the same path. That goes for this kitchen and the stairway, too. So please wait."

Lauren nodded. Osborne gave a silent sigh of relief, then said, "Chief Ferris, are you there?"

"Doc," asked Lew, "is that someone at the Ericsson house?"

"Yes, I just informed Lauren Crowell, the Ericsson campaign manager, of the situation. She said that during their campaign layovers she has been staying here but she's aware of why she has to leave. I was just about to help her get her things—"

"No, Doc. Not yet. Please have her wait for me to get there. Should be there in less than ten minutes—and do your best to keep the site as pristine as possible."

"Will do. There is a side entry from the driveway, which is all I've used. I'll see that nothing more is disturbed."

"I'm trying to get there before any media show up. I can't keep a lid on the news of Jane's death much longer. You know this is going to be a helluva circus.

By the way, how's she handling it?"

"Pretty well. So far." Osborne glanced at Lauren. "Taking some time to sink in."

"Think she's capable of answering a few questions before we move her?"

"My guess is yes, but that could change."

"We'll give it a try. And, Doc, you don't mind staying to help with the interrogation, I hope. I know Mallory and her friend need—"

"Not a problem, Lew. I'll be here." During Osborne's first stint as the deputy coroner for the Loon Lake Police Department, Lew had discovered he could be an unexpected asset during the questioning of suspects. The reason? Men and women hear differently. Depending on the listener—emotions, facts, even words can have ambiguous meanings. More than once each had surprised the other with an interpretation of a response that changed the direction of the investigation.

Osborne checked his phone and saw a text from Mallory. "Excuse me," he said to Lauren, who had sat back down on her stool. "I need to make one more call."

"Obviously I'm not moving until you say so," said Lauren. Her snide tone made it clear she was not used to taking orders.

Chapter Twelve

Four miles from where Osborne and Lauren Crowell were awaiting Lew's arrival, Ray's pontoon was drifting along the outer edge of the weed bed in the northwest corner of Loon Lake. Mallory watched as Kenton cast his lure so close to Ray's line that it nearly snagged it.

"Kenton, be careful," she said, trying not to sound critical, "you really shouldn't cast so close to someone else's line."

"But he's caught two fish on that side of the boat," said Kenton, "and I haven't got anything on this side."

"Nevertheless, it's bad manners to do that," said Mallory. She refrained from mentioning that skill might have something to do with catching a fish.

"Manners? You go fishing and have to mind your manners?" said Kenton. "You must be kidding. I don't worry about manners on the basketball court—I go for the ball. Here, I'm gonna go for the fish. Right, Ray?"

"Mallory has a point," said Ray. "Now . . . I realize you've never fished before, so you are excused this time. But for the record, yes, there have been books written about the proper etiquette among fishermen. Don't want to get shot, dontcha know." He grinned at Kenton. "But Mallory wants you to have a good time, so you go right ahead and take my spot."

Ray reeled in his lure and stepped back. He looked over at Christina, who was casting off the opposite side with a slight breeze behind her. "I'll fish over here with my lovely lady friend. She's got a line I'd like to cross ..." Ray's double entendre hit home as Christina gave him a sidelong glance. Watching the two, Mallory suspected he had already crossed that line. A hint of jealousy stirred in her heart.

She glanced over at Kenton. He was trying, she had to give him that. Ray had banged on the bedroom window at six that morning and hustled them over to his trailer, where he and Christina had packed up a cooler with sandwiches and hot coffee. Not long after they got on the lake, Christina had hooked a large northern pike. Since then, Ray had caught and released two small walleyes.

"Whoa!" Kenton lurched forward, nearly falling over the pontoon railing. "Got something! Oh my God, what do I do now?" he cried, flailing with his rod over his head as the fish charged the boat.

"Tighten that line," said Ray as he set down his rod to stand alongside Kenton. "That's good .. now let some out ... remember what I told you about drag ... okay, now reel it in ... good, keep it coming."

"Maybe you'd better take over?" Kenton asked Ray. It was the first time Mallory had ever heard Kenton sound uncertain.

"N-o-o-o," said Ray, "you're going to do this ..."

Minutes later, Kenton held high a twenty-eight-inch walleye. "That is one of the biggest walleye I have ever seen caught in Loon Lake," said Ray. "Let Christina take a picture for you."

"Maybe I should have it mounted?" asked Kenton, eager as an eight-year-old with his first big catch.

Mallory laughed, happy to see Kenton so pleased. "That would look pretty cool on your office wall."

Kenton turned to her with a big grin. "You are right. Great idea, sweetie." It was the nicest thing he had said to her all day. Maybe tonight he would roll over to her side of the bed.

From deep inside one of the pontoon's storage units where Ray had stashed her backpack, Mallory heard the muffled ring of a cell phone. She raised the lid and grabbed for her phone.

"Oh, hi, Dad, yeah. We're out here with Ray, and Kenton just got a huge walleye—what? Oh, my gosh, that's awful. Yes, Ray is right here. I'll put him on."

She handed the cell phone to Ray, who listened, his face serious, as Osborne spoke. "Sure, Doc, I should be there within half an hour. No, Christina needs to leave soon anyway. Not a problem." He clicked off the phone and handed it back to Mallory.

"What is it?" asked Christina.

"Jane Ericsson has been found murdered," said Ray.

All three people on the pontoon stared at him, speechless. "Chief Ferris needs me at the Ericsson property. Wants me to search the grounds. Sorry, folks, but our fishing is over. Kenton, I'll clean that walleye for you after I shoot a photo. You can take it to a taxidermist I know and have a mount made. May be kind of pricey though."

As Ray maneuvered the pontoon up to his dock, Mallory spotted the figure of an older woman at the door to Ray's trailer. She was carrying a shopping bag, which she hung on the door latch.

"Kaye, wait," said Ray, hollering up at her. "I heard the news."

Kaye walked a short distance toward the dock and paused to wave back toward the trailer. "Got your hat done. Can't talk now. Too much to do." She sounded weary.

"Poor Kaye," said Ray to Mallory. "Jane Ericsson was her family—all the family she had left. They had their spats but . . ." He shook his head and turned to help Christina and Mallory off the pontoon.

Kenton had jumped onto the dock and was checking his phone for e-mails. "Hey, Mallory," he said without looking up from the phone, "I want to follow Ray over to the Ericsson place. This is a catastrophe the media will inhale. Has to be worth a hundred grand in crisis communications. That campaign manager must be going nuts. How far away is the place?"

Chapter Thirteen

As Lew turned down Rolf Ericsson Drive, she checked the rear view mirror and grimaced. The Channel 12 television crew was right behind her cruiser. She knew it had to happen, but darn, she had hoped to get through the morning before dealing with the questions she couldn't answer.

She pulled to a stop as soon as the old Ericsson lodge and the new house with its bright red roof were in view. She got out and walked back to the van. A young man she had never seen before thrust a microphone at her, but she reached out to put a hand over it.

"Not yet, young man. I will have a statement for the media this afternoon at three—"

"But—" The reporter yanked his mike out of her hand.

"No 'buts' about it," said Lew. "It's too early in our investigation for us to give you factual information. Hope to have something later, like I said. Right now you may not enter this property any further. Do you hear me? This may be a crime scene. If your driver crosses this line—" Lew drew an imaginary line in front of the van's left tire. "—you will all be arrested."

The reporter closed his eyes in frustration, then said, "One thing, okay? We're here first. Right? When you're ready, will you talk to us first, please?"

Lew thought that over, then said, "I have a suggestion. We passed a field back a ways. Why don't you park there? Tell any more press who come that they should line up behind you. I will talk to everyone at once, but you will be in the front."

The reporter leaned back into the van and said to someone with him, "Sounds good to me. We'll get good video. Okay, agreed. Say, Chief Ferris," he said as the van driver put the vehicle in reverse, "I heard you found human body parts?"

"Good try," said Lew. "Later."

Doc and a tall, dark-haired woman were waiting for her in the kitchen of the new house." Lauren Crowell, this is Loon Lake Police Chief Lewellyn Ferris," said Osborne as she walked into the airy room.

"Lauren Crowell," said the woman, "I'm managing Jane Ericsson's Senate campaign—or what's left of it anyway."

"Dr. Osborne filled you in on what we found early this morning?" asked Lew.

Lauren nodded. "Still not sure I believe it. But I want to give you all the help I can."

"Good. Let's take a seat over there," said Lew, walking to a sitting area in the living room that held three small black leather sofas facing each other with a round coffee table in front of them. She gave a quick look around the high-ceilinged space. "Quite a place, huh." She set a digital recorder on the coffee table, turned it on, and identified the three people who would be participating.

"Miss Crowell, I understand that in addition to being the campaign manager for the victim, Jane Ericsson, that you have been residing here at her home. Correct?"

"First, please call me Lauren. Yes, but it would be more accurate to say that I stay over here when traveling in the area. I'm a guest, not a resident. My home is in Washington, D.C."

"Why are you here now?" asked Lew.

"Last night was supposed to be a pontoon party, a fundraiser for the campaign in Madison, with seven couples, all of whom are major donors. I was there, waiting for Jane to arrive. When she didn't show, I drove up here as fast as I could. Got here around four this morning."

"What time was she due to arrive in Madison?"

"Five o'clock. We had things to go over. Usually she flies down in a small jet that she owns, but her pilots said she didn't show up and she didn't answer their phone calls. They figured she must have decided to drive down. She's done that more than once when she needs a break from people. We all learned a long time ago not to argue with Jane." Lauren gave a small smile.

"Why didn't you call the authorities when she didn't show up? Weren't you worried?"

"Great question. Ranks up there with 'why don't trees touch the sky?'" Again Osborne heard the brittle laugh.

When neither Lew nor Osborne responded, she sat up straighter, her face somber as she said, "Jane has ... had ... a drinking problem. It got worse in the last few weeks. The pressure of the campaign, maybe? If she had pulled over to sleep or stopped in a bar on the way down, I didn't want the press to know. You have no idea how many times I might have called the cops, only to have her show up within a couple hours. You don't want to be the person who cries 'wolf' too many times. Right?" Lauren slumped back against the sofa.

"Even if this has happened before," said Lew, "how long were you planning to wait before ..." She paused, then said, "Never mind. I have more important questions for you right now. For the record, our session will be brief and I'll need to talk with you again later. Right now, I need a few facts before I leave you to find temporary lodging. Has Dr. Osborne explained that this property is off limits until the team from the Wausau Crime Lab has completed their work?"

"Yes, and how long do you expect that to take?" asked Lauren.

"I have no idea. Depends on what they find. But I expect them out here shortly. Now, going back to my questions. And Dr. Osborne may have some as well."

"Of course," said Lauren, folding her arms and sitting back on the sofa.

"How long have you known Jane Ericsson?" asked Lew.

"Two years. We started working on this campaign almost exactly one year ago."

"In Washington, D.C.?"

"Actually, no. We were in Madison when it started to come together."

"Madison?" asked Osborne. "Are you from Wisconsin?"

"Yes. I grew up in Presque Isle."

"And *how* did you meet Jane?" he asked.

"The usual Wisconsin way," said Lauren with a slight smile as she picked at an imaginary piece of lint on one knee. "We were at a bar, and friends introduced us. We, just, well, we hit it off right away. I was lobbying at the time for an out-of-state microbrewery, so we chatted about politics, and one thing led to another. She told me about her family, her father and his amazing career. I encouraged her to run for the Senate. I told her I *knew* she could win."

Lauren's eyes brimmed and she pushed a Kleenex at her nose. "None of this would have happened if I hadn't pushed Jane to run . . ."

"Were you a couple?" asked Lew.

"Oh, no. 'Course, I think that old biddy next door thought we were."

"Why would she think that?" asked Osborne, surprised.

"Because I made Jane stop having her over all the time. When I first started coming here that woman just dropped in whenever. I couldn't believe it."

"They have known each other since they were youngsters," said Osborne. "People up here drop in on one another. It's the way we are. I'm sure it's the same in Presque Isle."

"Well, she didn't make a good impression on other guests," said Lauren. "Jane and I made it a point to entertain influential people who might donate to the campaign and Kaye . . . Do you know her? She's weird—old, scruffy." Lauren shuddered. "Not the image we've been working to project."

"How was Jane to work for?" asked Lew. "You said she had a drinking problem. Could she be abusive?"

"No, heavens, no. We got along great. She approved the strategy I brought her, the staff I hired. We had a great working relationship until . . ."

"Until when?" Lew kept her tone even.

"Oh, we just disagreed over that Kaye Lund person, but Jane got over it. I mean, you can't work side by side every day and not have a few issues."

"True," said Lew.

"It might be good for you to know that Kaye Lund is organizing a memorial service for people here in Loon Lake," said Osborne.

"Oh, no, she won't. I'll take care of that. Things are bad enough without her setting up some rinky-dink affair." Lauren reached for the cell phone that she had set down beside her on the sofa. She hit several buttons, waited, and when there was no answer gave a sigh of irritation as she set the phone down. "Damn, the old frog never answers."

"I would like to suggest that, given the grim circumstances we have at the moment, you consider deferring to Kaye," said Osborne, finding himself anxious to protect Kaye, who was hardly a match for the sophisticated, harsh-voiced woman sitting across from him. "Whether you like her or not, she and Jane have been like family for years."

What he didn't say was that Kaye's grief mattered, too. No matter what Lauren Crowell might think, Kaye had a right to bury her "summer sister."

The sound of a car honking off in the distance reminded Lew of her conversation with the television crew. "Doc," she said, turning to Osborne, who was seated to her right, "as I drove in here I was followed by the first of what I expect to be many television crews and other media. I've got a call in to the sheriff for help with traffic and all the hoopla that's sure to happen before this day is over. I've no doubt they'll camp out here and in front of the department. Do you think Mallory would be willing to help me out with a press release, and maybe find some way to keep all those reporters out of our way?"

"Who is Mallory?" asked Lauren.

"My daughter, who is visiting from Chicago," said Osborne. "Erin's older sister. She works for a marketing firm. Her MBA is in marketing, but her undergrad degree was in journalism from Northwestern. Sure, Chief, I can ask her if she'd help out."

"Wait," said Lauren, leaning forward as she spoke. "With Jane gone, I'm now the spokesperson for the campaign. I should be handling the media. I mean—is there any reason I can't?"

"You certainly cannot speak for law enforcement and this investigation," said Lew.

"I don't mean that," said Lauren, "but I'll be under a lot of pressure trying to explain how Jane's death will affect the party, not to mention the campaign. Please, this campaign is a twenty-million-dollar operation—"

"Excuse me, Lauren," said Osborne, "there are two separate issues to consider here. One is the investigation; the other is the fallout from the death of a prominent politician in the midst of running for office. The media will be after answers from both camps. Right?"

"What a nightmare this will be," said Lew, shaking her head.

"You haven't seen anything yet," said Lauren. "The moment this news hits the Internet, Loon Lake be inundated. Chief Ferris, you better be prepared for reporters from TV, newspapers, radio, the Internet. The roads around Loon Lake will be clogged with press."

"Making it difficult to do my job," said Lew.

"On the other hand," said Lauren with a shrug, "the minute something awful happens somewhere else, they'll disappear. In an instant. Just watch."

"So I should hope that someone else has bad luck?"

Lauren raised her eyebrows as she said, "Hate to say it, but that wouldn't hurt."

"Well, I'll deal with that when I have to. Doc, you talk to Mallory about the media assistance that I will need. Lauren, I understand your need to answer questions relating to the campaign—but *only* the campaign."

"You have my word. I know the legal implications." Assuming the session was over, Lauren grabbed her phone and got to her feet.

"No," said Lew, directing her to sit down again. "If you were in Madison last night, who were you with?"

"You mean like I need an alibi?"

"Everyone in this region who knew Jane Ericsson will need an alibi."

"Most of the evening I was at the home of Chuck Winters, who was hosting the pontoon party—one of Jane's top donors. And I had dropped my overnight bag at the home of a good friend where I had planned to spend the night. Phyllis Cook is her name. Would you like a phone number?"

"Yes, please," said Lew.

"Let me get my purse. It's right over there on the counter," said Lauren. She got up, retrieved the purse, and reached in for a cardholder. Osborne noted that the number she recited to Lew had a Madison area code.

"Lauren," said Lew, "is there anyone you think might have a reason to have committed this crime?"

"Certainly not her opponent," said Lauren. "No one could be that stupid."

Lew gave a slight smile and waited.

"That's a tough question," said Lauren. "Gosh, I hate to target anyone . . . but, yes, I can think of two people in particular, but please promise you won't tell them I said so."

"Can't do that, I'm afraid," said Lew. "Now that you've said this much, you'll be guilty of withholding evidence if you don't tell me more."

"Oh, dear . . . okay, there's this guy, Mike Kelly, he's an environmental activist who hates Jane. She arranged a deal for a wetlands development outside Wausau and he's been stalking the campaign ever since. Drives an older-model dark green van. He's in his mid-thirties. You know, the Madison liberal type. And I have seen him at our rallies up here as recently as two weeks ago. But I cannot imagine he would go this far."

"Someone else?" asked Lew.

"Y-e-e-e-s . . ." Lauren checked over her shoulder as if she was afraid that someone was listening. She lowered her voice. "That crazy old woman next door."

"You mean Kaye Lund? Are you serious?" asked Osborne.

"Yes. This sounds absurd, I know, but she tried to blackmail Jane. Said that if Jane didn't pay her fifty thousand bucks that she would go public with the fact that when Jane was in her early thirties, right after her divorce, that she had an affair with a sixteen-year-old boy. Someone up here, in fact." As she spoke, Lew caught Osborne's eye.

"Jane told her she was crazy and kicked her out of the house. Unfortunately, she threatened Kaye to her face, too."

"How so?" asked Lew.

"I'm not sure, but something about changing her will so Kaye would have to move out of that old house she lives in."

"Are you sure about all that?" asked Osborne. "I heard a version of this story, but I thought it was the other way around. That Jane decided for whatever reasons to sever the friendship she and Kaye have had for years. I heard it was after Jane treated her badly that Kaye was thinking of going public with the story of the affair. She never has. Not yet anyway."

"Ha, that's a crock," said Lauren. "Whatever you think you heard, Dr. Osborne, that's all wrong."

"It's not what I *think* I heard," said Osborne, "I know what I heard. You realize you are accusing Kaye Lund of murder? I've known Kaye for years and I can't imagine her threatening blackmail. You better have that story straight . . ."

Maybe it was the late morning sun streaming through the high windows, but Osborne thought he saw Lauren's eyes glitter, shards of yellow flickering in the dark irises. She hesitated before closing her eyes and saying, "You may be right and I got it wrong. The whole scene that night was just so upsetting to me." Lauren paused before saying, "I should never have said a word."

A loud knocking at the side door was followed by a man's voice. "Chief Ferris? Bruce Peters here. Are you inside? Okay to come in?"

Jumping to her feet, Lew rushed through the kitchen, saying, "Bruce, hold on. I'll be right there." Osborne was about to get up from the sofa and follow her when he saw Lauren lean forward, pick up the digital recorder and hit a button.

"Oh, no," she said with an apologetic smile. "So sorry—I just wanted to look at the brand of this recorder because I need a new one—and I'm afraid I hit delete."

Chapter Fourteen

Bruce followed as Osborne and Lew escorted Lauren to the bedroom and bathroom that she had been using, to gather up her things. They retraced their steps to the kitchen and out to the driveway, watching as Lauren loaded everything into her Jeep.

"Lauren," said Lew, "would you like my staff to make a call to the Northwoods Inn and reserve a room for you?"

"Thank you, I would appreciate that," said Lauren. As they were standing in the driveway while Lew gave Lauren directions to the inn, Ray arrived in his pickup with Christina beside him. Right behind Ray were Mallory and Kenton in the rental car.

"Chief Ferris," said Ray, "where do you want me to start?"

"You'll be working on your own, I hope," said Lew, with a look of concern at his companion.

"Oh, don't worry about Christina. She's riding back to my place with Mallory and Sparky over there. I wanted her to see the outside of this place, though. Isn't it amazing?"

"Wow, is it ever," said Christina, stepping back to get a full view of the house. A curious expression crossed her face and she stepped forward toward Lauren. "Hello, don't I know you from somewhere?"

"No," said Lauren, opening her car door. "I've never seen you before." As she got into the driver's seat, Christina said, "But I'm sure—"

"You're wrong," said Lauren, with a lilt in her voice. "Happens to me all the time—I must look like lots of people." Osborne couldn't help thinking that wasn't likely. In all his sixty-three years, he hadn't seen a woman looking the least bit like Lauren Crowell. But, he admitted to himself, it could be argued that he didn't get to the big city much either.

"Hey, Crowell, wait!" shouted Kenton as he leapt from the rental car to run across the driveway toward Lauren's Jeep. "I need to talk to you for a minute." He tried yanking open the car door. Lauren hit the unlock button, and Kenton pulled open the door. Osborne half expected him to grab Lauren by the arm and drag her from the car.

He didn't have to. She jumped out, and faced him, hands on her hips, saying, "How the hell did *you* get here?"

The anger in her voice surprised Lew, who had been about to follow Ray into the house. She stopped and turned.

"I'm staying with friends," said Kenton, pointing toward Mallory, who was standing beside the rental car. "Just heard the terrible news about Jane Ericsson, and I know you'll need help managing the media, the campaign—"

"We're fine." Lauren shut him down. "I've got staff—"

"Sure you do, but you've got a multimillion-dollar campaign to salvage. You need to focus on finding a substitute candidate, and let us handle crisis communications. I can have a proposal to you—" Kenton checked his watch "—by four o'clock today."

"No, thank you. I have everything under control." Lauren slid back under the steering wheel of the Jeep.

"I beg your pardon, but I don't think you realize there's half a dozen reporters already waiting right outside the entrance to this road," said Kenton. "You'll have five times that many within a few hours. What if I say we'll do half the job pro bono—"

Lauren said loudly through the open window, "What is it about 'N.O.' that you don't understand? No, no, and no."

"But I don't think you—"

"Buddy—" She shook a finger at him."—you have been warned. Now get out of my way, or I will run you over."

"You know—I believe you will," said Kenton, backing away. "And, lady," he said, derision dripping from his voice, "I don't think you have any idea what you are doing." Lauren's window shot up as he spoke. Spinning her wheels, she backed out, forcing Kenton to jump out of the way. As the Jeep drove off, Kenton marched toward Mallory. "Who the hell does that bitch think she is, anyway? She has to answer to someone. I'm going to find out who."

"I think that might be a fruitless search," said Lew from where she had been watching the exchange. Kenton gave her a dirty look, crossed his arms over his chest, and leaned back against the rental car, fuming.

Lew beckoned to Mallory. "I have a favor to ask, but I'm afraid it could ruin your vacation. Any chance you would be willing to work with Dani Fortier in my office to help her prepare statements for the press, and organize a press conference for myself and Bruce Peters from the Wausau Crime Lab? Dani is great with the basics. She knows the computer system and our public affairs policies, but she's no expert in media relations, and I can't delay addressing the media much longer. Problem is, I have no budget for media relations. Would you consider volunteering?"

Before Mallory could answer, Kenton rushed up. "I'll handle it. This is right in my wheelhouse."

"I didn't ask you," said Lew, her voice kind but firm. "I asked Mallory."

"Chief Ferris, I am more than happy to help out," said Mallory. She glanced sideways at Kenton. "If it's okay with you, Kenton will, too."

"But I want you in charge," said Lew. "You and Dani—she knows our protocol. I'll call the station and tell her to expect you."

"Sure," said Mallory. "After we drop off Christina, I'll head for town right away. Kenton was right, you have a crowd gathering out on the main road, so we need to tackle the media right away. Kenton, you want to come along?"

Kenton, his face a storm cloud, said, "Of course, I'm coming along. I want to know just who that woman thinks she is." He threw himself back into the car.

As they drove back toward Ray's place, Christina said from the back seat, "Mallory, when you have a chance, please tell your dad and Chief Ferris that I am ninety-nine percent sure that woman, Lauren Crowell, was in my art gallery last month. One of my assistants caught her shoplifting several hundred dollars' worth of hair extensions."

"Are you sure?" asked Mallory, giving a quick glance over her shoulder.

"Pretty positive."

"Is she from up there?" asked Kenton.

"That I don't know. Never saw her before the incident in the store. She can be intimidating. Fortunately, we have a surveillance camera, so we had her on video. When my assistant stopped her outside the store, she said she 'forgot' she had them in her bag."

"Still have the tape?" asked Kenton.

"Afraid not. We erase every two days. I need a better system."

"We'll make sure to let Chief Ferris know," said Kenton. "I learned a long time ago when I was working as an investigative reporter that it's the bad habits people have that tell you everything about them. More accurate than a resume."

Chapter Fifteen

"So where are we right now?" Lew asked Bruce as she and Osborne joined him around the island in Jane Ericsson's kitchen.

"Got an update for you, but, boy oh boy, will you look at this kitchen," said Bruce. "This place is so clean it sparkles. Think anyone ever cooks here? Sorry, off the subject. Yes, I do have some news, but nothing great to go on.

"Talked to your water utility guy, Bert Gilligan, a couple hours ago, and he agreed to send a crew out to check all the storm sewers in town. Got back to me pretty fast to say the grate over the storm drain in the library parking lot had been moved recently. They could tell because it had wet leaves stuck along the edges, and it wasn't set in the way it should be.

"He also checked their map of the new storm sewer system and said that the flow from the sewers in that part of Loon Lake converges in the swamp on the east side, and is directed through culverts into the underground stream that flooded the past few days. From there the water flows straight into the Tomorrow River. Bert pointed out that under normal conditions there isn't enough flow to keep bundles like the ones we've found moving. He thinks—and I agree—that our suspect counted on the rain and the current to keep those bundles moving. If Stan hadn't been alert and a fan of frozen meat, we may never have known what happened to our victim."

"Interesting," said Lew. "Have you finished investigating the site on Woodland Avenue? If so, I'll have Todd and Roger knock on doors of the folks living near the library to see if they saw any vehicles or people in the parking lot."

"I'll be surprised if they did," said Bruce. "The condition of the body parts I've seen so far makes me think the victim died within the last twenty-four to thirty-six hours. I believe those bundles were dropped in the early, early morning hours Saturday morning when the rain was at its heaviest. Very likely they drove up to the sewer grate with their lights off. But it's worth a try, Chief.

"Yes, we're done at the Woodland site though we're going to leave it barricaded for a few days. We don't need the press trampling through there in case there's something we've missed. I hope you don't mind if I ask Ray Pradt to take a look, too."

"Of course not," said Lew. "I want him scouring the yard and woods here, too, in case someone has been hanging around outdoors, stalking the victim. I would like to be able to confirm that she was abducted from here."

"Good," said Bruce. "I did stop by the storefront downtown that's serving as a local headquarters for the campaign, but they said they hadn't seen Ericsson at all this week. So nothing there. After I get some lunch, I'll do this house and her car. Who lives next door? I noticed an old frame house at the end of the drive. Looks lived in."

"That belongs to Kaye Lund, and she's lived there for years," said Osborne. "She's a former employee of the Ericsson family and has known the victim for years."

"A suspect?" asked Bruce.

"Not likely," said Osborne, "though the campaign manager seems to think that because Kaye and Jane had a falling out recently, she could be. I've known Kaye for years and find it hard to believe that she would be capable of murdering a woman she cared for like a sister."

Bruce wrinkled his nose and shifted his dark eyebrows up and down before saying, "Yeah, well, let's see what I find here. But it sounds like I better put that place on my list."

"Do we have to ask her to move out?" asked Osborne.

Bruce walked back down the stairs to the side door to peer across the drive toward Kaye's place. "Give me a couple of hours. Let me see what I find here first."

"You can start right there," said Lew, pointing to the kitchen counter near a large Sub-Zero refrigerator. "That's Jane Ericsson's purse."

"Isn't that interesting," said Bruce. "That could mean she was abducted from here. I don't know many women who go anywhere without their purse."

"Mayor Tillman," said Lew, "I'm glad you could join us. I'd like you to meet Mallory Osborne, Doc's daughter. She organized this press conference for us. Hope you don't mind us using city hall, but we have quite a gathering of media that we need to accommodate."

"Oh, this is fine," said Chet Tillman, basking in the glow of the lights set up by the photographers and cameramen. He was wearing a dark pinstriped business suit, its authority undermined by a jacket straining to hide a belly that, Lew had whispered to Mallory, "entered the room before he did."

It had been Mallory's suggestion to include the mayor, given the intense attention from the press. But Lew, still smarting from his attempt six months earlier to force her into retirement in favor of appointing his son as chief, had hesitated. She detested the man. Just seeing him could ruin her day.

"Chief Ferris," Mallory had cajoled, "you need a good space with plenty of room for cameras and equipment. And the more people who can make a statement to the press, the less you have to talk. Bottom line: I'm afraid that if we want to use Loon Lake City Hall, we have to include the mayor."

That convinced Lew. She had been going since four that morning, and when she got fatigued, she got cranky. "Okay, give him the opening statement, then Bruce Peters from the Wausau Crime Lab, and I'll follow up."

She reminded herself that Chet Tillman Jr., on being caught making inappropriate remarks on his Facebook page, had voluntarily taken a position with the sheriff's department in Oconto County where he was sure to make more money. The good news was he saved face, and the old man let up on pushing for him to have the Loon Lake appointment—at least for the time being.

Lew turned her attention back to the preparations for the press conference. Loon Lake City Hall had been built of brownstone from the shores of Lake Superior in the late 1800s. While the building was in serious need of restoration, the interior was spacious with wide stairways, high ceilings and a city council meeting room that could accommodate over a hundred people.

Even though she had been warned, Lew was surprised at how many members of the media showed up: six television crews from the Wausau area with feeds into the national networks, and over a dozen reporters trailing photographers from publications ranging from the Internet's the *Huffington Post* to the *New York Times*, the *Wall Street Journal*, and the Associated Press, whose story would run nationally online.

The press conference moved at a brisk pace, with Mayor Tillman testifying to the community's shock at the nature of the crime and the prominence of the Ericsson family, including the guaranteed success that had been expected of Jane Ericsson's run for the U.S. Senate. Bruce spoke briefly of the investigation underway and underscored the current lack of leads. Lew picked up on that theme. She emphasized that the police were cooperating with the crime lab, and asked anyone in the community who might know something to please come forward.

"Why aren't the FBI involved?" asked one television reporter.

"They may work with us if we don't have a break soon," said Lew. "In that case we'll form a task force to work the evidence together. Right now this murder is under the jurisdiction of the Loon Lake Police. Crimes that fall under FBI jurisdiction include those in which the criminal crossed state lines, violations of federal controlled substance laws, and other violations of federal laws. We don't have any of those issues yet."

"Chief Ferris, I heard the body was cut up and packaged like they butcher deer—is that correct?" asked the reporter from the *Loon Lake Daily News*.

"The body was not intact," said Lew. "That is all I can say. We do not want to jeopardize the investigation, so please respect that."

Mallory stood at the back of the room with copies of a press release that contained statements from each of the speakers. As Lew and Bruce were answering questions from the reporters, she felt a tap on her shoulder. She turned to face a tired-looking woman in black jeans and a black T-shirt with short brown hair and no makeup, wearing a press badge that identified her as a reporter from the *New York Times*. The photo on the badge showed her with no makeup and wearing a black shirt: she matched the picture.

"Whoa, the *New York Times*. Boy, you got here fast—"

"Got a charter out of Minneapolis. I need to talk to that chief of police," said the woman before Mallory could finish.

"Sorry," said Mallory. "The statements made here are as much as the police and the crime lab want made public until they know more. Like everyone else, you'll just have to wait."

"No," said the woman, "this isn't about reporting. I have information that I think may be helpful in the investigation. I know a person who had a meeting with Jane Ericsson late Friday night and may have been one of the last people to see her alive—and I have reason to think that person's life is in danger."

The woman's intensity convinced Mallory. "Okay, wait here," she said. "I'll see what I can do."

The minute Lew stepped down from the podium where she had been standing with Tillman and Bruce, Mallory pulled her aside. In a low whisper, she repeated what the woman had said. "Be careful, Chief," she said, "you don't want speaking with her to look like you're giving an exclusive interview, or all hell will break loose."

"Good point," said Lew. "But I've got television crews and reporters hanging around the station, too. Any suggestions?"

Mallory puzzled over the situation, then said, "I'll give her directions to Dad's house. You can speak privately there."

"Good. Will you tell your dad what I'm doing and why, and ask him to please meet me there?"

"Done." Pushing sideways through the crowd and stepping over bags of camera equipment, Mallory edged her way to the rear of the room. She motioned to the reporter. "Meet Chief Ferris here as soon as you can," she said. She handed the reporter a slip of paper with Osborne's address. "Do you need a map?"

"No. I can use my phone," the woman choked and Mallory thought for a second that she would burst into tears. "Be there in ten minutes. By the way—my name is Wendy Marron."

"Mallory Osborne—" But the reporter didn't hear her. She was dashing down the stairs toward the exit from city hall.

Twenty minutes later, Lew and Osborne were standing in his kitchen with the reporter from the *Times*.

"Dr. Osborne, Chief Ferris, I'm Wendy Marron, environmental reporter for the *New York Times*, which is why I was contacted by this guy, Mike Kelly, from Madison. He's very involved with an environmental group working to maintain the state's wetlands, and he has been trying to convince Jane Ericsson, if she was elected, to block a business venture outside Wausau that is threatening to fill in over one hundred acres of pristine wetlands.

"Last month, Kelly's group received a grant of fifty thousand dollars for their work. They decided to use the money to convince the Ericsson campaign to support their cause, in return for a donation."

"Of fifty thousand dollars?" asked Lew.

"Yes, but on the condition that Jane Ericsson herself agreed to meet with Kelly. When she heard how much money was involved, her staff set up the meeting. That meeting was supposed to be late this past Friday night at Jane Ericsson's home here in Loon Lake. I've been told that she agreed to accept the donation so long as it was in cash—"

"In cash? That's strange," said Osborne. "Why wouldn't a check be more appropriate?"

"That was a red flag for me, too," said Wendy. "Kelly said that Jane Ericsson told him she wanted to be sure that the developer—who thought they had a deal—couldn't trace the donation and accuse her of taking a bribe."

"But she *was* taking a bribe," said Lew.

"Of course she was. Or he thought she was. Now, while I never met Mike Kelly in person, I have spoken to him on the phone and he e-mailed me all the particulars. His plan was to show up, offer the money, and use his cell phone to video the exchange. He was planning to send me and several other reporters the video immediately afterwards."

"So the national media would have Jane Ericsson on tape accepting a bribe from a constituent . . ."

"Exactly. I tried to discourage him, because the whole thing didn't make sense. Why would a politician of Ericsson's caliber risk her campaign for such a modest amount of money? But Kelly wouldn't listen, he's a fanatic. He is so determined to stop the development, to save the wetlands—he would do anything. You know, the guy doesn't strike me as having a lot of common sense. But that's beside the point right now.

"Something went wrong, because his girlfriend called me late yesterday, just frantic. He's disappeared. She keeps trying his cell phone, but there's no answer. I thought you should know. I mean, the guy has fifty thousand dollars in cash on him . . . where the hell is he?"

"Can you reach the girlfriend?" asked Lew. "Find out what company he uses for his cell phone, the number, everything she knows. I'll see if I can put through a trace on his phone right now."

"Don't you need a subpoena for that?"

"Not for a rescue. A missing person is not a missing felon. Maybe it turns out he ran off with the money, maybe he met with Jane Ericsson and something went so wrong he killed her, maybe, maybe. But right now I am focused on a person who has gone missing in Loon Lake, and whose life may be at stake. You seem to think so—right?" Lew asked Wendy.

"I do. I may think the guy's a fanatic, but I do believe his heart is in the right place. If he wanted to steal that money, he didn't have to drive up here and wait for that woman."

"You're sure he did?"

"He texted me from her driveway. Told me to stand by, 'cause he planned to e-mail the video within the hour."

Chapter Sixteen

Ray knocked on Kaye Lund's screen door and waited. The afternoon sun was hot on his back, and he noticed the windows along the front of the house had been shoved wide open. After waiting a good minute, he knocked again as he said, "Hello, Kaye? It's Ray. Need a little help here. Helloooo, anybody home?"

From the darkened room beyond the screen door, a shadow lumbered toward him. With a creak of the hinges, Kaye pushed the door open and beckoned him inside. Her cheeks were damp and her eyes red-rimmed. A balled-up handkerchief that may have been white in a previous life was clutched in one hand. Raising the hanky to her face, she blew her nose long and hard.

"I am so sorry to bother you, Kaye. What an awful time this must be."

"'S fine. You get your hat okay? I left it at your place."

"Hat's great, Kaye. I'll betcha I can wear it for another ten years. Thank you, but that's not—"

"I got the memorial service all set for Tuesday morning," said Kaye. "Father John's gonna say a funeral Mass even though we may not have a casket ..." A sob escaped in spite of her effort to keep her voice level. A quick wipe of the handkerchief at her face, and she managed to force more words out. "Father said it's okay 'cause it'll be kind of like a cremation, y'know? And, um, I've arranged for the church ladies to have lunch for everyone afterwards."

"Isn't that rushing things?" asked Ray, his voice soft. He didn't want to sound critical, but he wasn't sure Kaye was thinking clearly. "I mean—Tuesday is only two days from now."

He could have kicked himself the minute after he spoke. What was he thinking? That Jane's poor body would somehow reassemble itself for a traditional viewing, Mass, and burial? Chances were the crime lab might not release the remains for months. Kaye's effort might lend some decency, if not respect, to the grim developments around Jane Ericsson's death.

"Father John is going fishing in Canada on Thursday. He said it has to be Tuesday or not for another couple weeks. I thought maybe it would be good to get it over with. You know all those college kids that were working for Jane this summer. Be nice if they can attend. Don't you think? Oh, Ray, did I do the wrong thing?" The despair in Kaye's eyes broke his heart.

"No, of course not. If Father John thinks it's okay, then I'm sure he's right. But you shouldn't have to pay for the luncheon. Think how many people may come—hundreds, perhaps."

"I hope so," said Kaye, her voice shaking as she started to break down. "That," she sobbed, "... that would make Jane so happy."

Kaye's head fell forward, her shoulders shaking. Uncertain what to do next, Ray pulled one of the kitchen chairs up next to the rocker and sat down. He placed a reassuring hand on her knee as he said, "Let me help organize the memorial and the luncheon. You know, Doc's daughter is visiting, and she can help, too. And I know lots of people who will be happy to chip in a few bucks for the luncheon. For heaven's sake, Kaye, Jane's estate must be worth millions. Whoever manages it should help pay for the luncheon, too."

"Now, Ray, you listen to me," said Kaye. She paused to blow her nose and wipe at her eyes. Clearing her throat, she sat up straight in the rocker, her chin thrust forward. "Jane was all the family I had. We might have had a little falling out last month, but that was just because of the hoopla 'round the campaign. I know it wasn't her who got so mad at me. Not really. It was that awful woman she hired. Goddamn spider, that woman."

Kaye was rocking back and forth with such vengeance, Ray had to reach out and slow her down. When she came to a stop, she leveled her eyes at him, saying, "I am doing this my way, and I don't want you telling anyone. Promise me you'll keep your mouth shut?" Her tone softened. "It's my last chance to take care of little sis."

Ray got to his feet and patted her shoulder. "I won't tell a soul, but I insist you let me know if you need help. You promise me that and we've got a deal."

Kaye managed a slight smile. "Deal."

"Good, that's taken care of. But, Kaye, the reason I dropped by is I need a pair of your shoes. Chief Ferris wants me to check the grounds around the property for any sign of an intruder. The ground is so soft from the rain, especially around the house where no shrubs have been planted yet. I need to be able to tell your footprints from any stranger's."

"Oh, that makes sense," said Kaye, pushing her heavy body up from the rocker, "but you better check with some of the workmen who've been around, too. Hold on, I'll get you something you can use." She walked into the kitchen where she leaned down to reach for a pair of black rubber boots. "Here, I always wear these when I'm outside gardening. Will these work?"

A siren wail in the distance drew closer. In less than a minute, a large SUV driven by Randy Kucsmarek, one of the sheriff's deputies, came hurtling down the drive past the big house and skidded to a stop in the clearing in front of Kaye's house. Right behind the SUV was Osborne's Subaru.

The deputy jumped from the driver's seat and ran up to where Ray and Kaye stood watching him. "Hey, Pradt," he said, "they got a signal from a cell phone belonging to some guy who's gone missing for three days. The signal is coming from somewhere in the woods between Rolf Ericsson Drive and the county road. Chief Ferris wants you and Doc Osborne to check it out. See what you can find. If you need help or want to use our K-9 search and rescue dog, give a call. I'm outta here now, though—we got a heck of a problem managing all the idiots driving in to see where the body parts were found. What a circus." He shook his head in disgust, and climbed back into his vehicle.

"Kaye, how's it going? Sorry to disrupt you like this," said Osborne after the deputy had driven off.

"I'm ... managing." As Kaye spoke, they heard a loud bang from the back of the house. "Jeez, what's that? Sounds like my back door." Before she could walk back into the kitchen, Lauren Crowell came flying into the front room.

"What the hell do you think you're doing?" she said, looming over Kaye.

"None of your business," said Kaye, sounding smug as she walked back over to her rocking chair.

Lauren threw an angry look at Osborne and Ray, who were standing speechless. "She's made arrangements for Jane's funeral. Got the whole damn town coming to a party. *What's that all about?*"

"We call it a wake," said Kaye, starting to rock. "That's what we do here when someone passes away."

Lauren sputtered. "I know what a wake is. Don't tell me what a wake is. I want a national memorial service for a woman who might have become a U.S. senator, not lunch in a fast food joint."

"St. Mary's school cafeteria is not a fast food joint." Kaye tipped her head higher as she spoke.

Lauren turned to Osborne. "Dr. Osborne, you tell her. It is so tacky to do this."

"Actually, Lauren," said Osborne, "I agree with Kaye. Loon Lake needs to mourn its own in its Northwoods way. I would imagine you can arrange another service on a larger stage when it's appropriate. Maybe in a month or two, in Madison or Washington, D.C. Something with status, like you say. But what Kaye is doing is right for here and now."

Lauren threw her hands into the air, spun around, and stomped through the kitchen and out the back door. The living room was silent except for a whisper of wood on rug as Kaye rocked. "Kaye, don't you lock your doors?" asked Osborne.

"Never. This is Loon Lake, Doc. Do you lock your doors?"

"Now that you mention it, no. But I have a dog."

Kaye shrugged and smiled. Ray and Osborne smiled back, their mutual satisfaction one ray of light in a somber day.

Chapter Seventeen

After placing Kaye's boots on the passenger seat in his pickup, Ray walked over to Osborne's car. "Doc, you know where this signal is coming from?" Before Osborne could answer, he said, "Poor Kaye. That woman has aged ten years since we saw her yesterday. And what is the deal with that Lauren woman? Does she need meds?"

"Lauren Crowell was running Jane's campaign and apparently she believes she is running everything around here. Just be happy she's not in the car with me. But yes, I've got a marked map with me that gives us some idea—"

"Is this connected to the Ericsson murder in some way? I can't imagine Lew would pull me off that search of the grounds if it wasn't."

"Not sure. All we know so far is that this Kelly fellow has been tag-teaming the campaign trying to get Jane to change her position on a wetland development project. His girlfriend got in touch with a reporter he was e-mailing to say he hasn't been heard from since Friday night, when he supposedly had a meeting with Jane at her home. The girlfriend is convinced he's lost or drowned or something." Osborne raised his eyebrows as he said, "Oh, I forgot to mention—the guy was carrying fifty thousand dollars in cash."

"In cash? What was this? A drug deal?"

"Who knows. He told the girlfriend it was to be a donation to the campaign that would encourage Jane to support his cause. V-e-r-y fishy. On the other hand, the guy was a fanatic on the issue, and this is politics."

"True," said Ray. "But hauling around fifty grand in cash is a good way to encourage a Jack Pine savage to support his wish for breaking your legs. So tell me again—exactly where are we going?"

"Got it right here," said Osborne reaching for the plat book on the passenger seat. "Want to remind you of one thing, in case that sheriff's deputy shows up again. Lew has not told anyone Mike Kelly's real reason for being up here but you, me, and Mallory. She wants to run this like a rescue search for a missing tourist. If it's a search for a suspect, she has to get a subpoena for the phone trace, and that could take a couple days."

"Chief Ferris strikes again," said Ray with a conspiratorial smile. "You sure she's not smarter 'n you are, Doc?"

"Thank you," said Osborne. "I'll remember that remark when you need a referral to a good endodontist. Okay, here we go," he said as he held the open plat book so that Ray could see the page. "The trace on the signal shows that it's somewhere within this area." Osborne pointed to a circle drawn on a map. "Can't pinpoint any closer than this—we have to search on foot."

"Hmm," said Ray, studying the map. "You know where this is, don't you?"

"I know there's a couple of logging roads back in there. Doesn't this land belong to the paper mill?"

"Doc, that's the old town dump," said Ray. "Been closed for years. My buddies and I used to ride our bikes back in there to watch the bears."

"You're right. I forgot about that. Okay, since you know the area, I'll follow you."

Back on the county road, Ray watched for signs of an old logging lane he knew was likely to lead back into the area marked on the plat map. A faint impression in an overgrown ditch along the highway looked promising. He pulled over.

"Doc, you better ride with me. This Subaru of yours rides so low you might get stuck."

"Good idea," said Osborne, reaching for his black bag. He hurried over to Ray's truck and opened the driver's side door. "Mind letting me slide in from your side?"

"Oh, sure," said Ray. "Sorry. Always forget that other door doesn't work."

Carefully, very carefully, Osborne slid under the steering wheel, past the gearshift, and into the passenger seat—where he reminded himself to be sure to take it slow getting out.

Scanning the dense growth of young aspen squeezing in on both sides of the narrow lane, Ray yanked the steering wheel back and forth, maneuvering the pickup over and around deep, muddy ruts. "Someone's been driving in here recently," he said, braking to a stop. "Hold on, Doc; before we go any further, I see something I want to check out."

Brushing back clumps of grass obscuring the faint outlines of the logging lane, Ray knelt for a closer look at tire patterns that had been left in the mud. He peered through the driver's side window of the truck. "We better park here, Doc," he said. "Whoever drove in here did so before the rain stopped. We'll go the rest of the way on foot, so we don't mess up any tracks."

"You mean a vehicle went in, but hasn't come out?"

"Not unless there's another way out, and I don't believe there is. Let's see that map again."

Osborne handed over the plat book, and Ray studied it for a long minute. "Okay," he said, looking up, "I'm going to bet we are within a thousand feet of that cell phone signal. Follow me and stay to the right, so we'll know those are our tracks."

"Got it," said Osborne.

The green VW van was parked in a clearing five hundred feet ahead. Behind it was all that remained of the old dump: a rusted iron fence, a wooden shack with its roof caved in, and a large berm capped with NO TRESPASSING signs. The afternoon might be warm and sunny, but the view of the dump was desolate. Nor did the sight of the van do anything positive to Osborne's gut.

Mike Kelly appeared to be dozing in the front seat of his van— head back, eyes half-open. Anticipating movement, Osborne and Ray approached slowly. But the man remained still. The window on the driver's side was open, and Osborne could hear flies buzzing. Up close, it was obvious Mike Kelly was deep into the sleep of the dead.

"Ray," said Osborne, pulling open his instrument bag, "let me give you a pair of nitrile gloves before you touch anything. Tell you right now—Bruce just got another couple days of work."

"Wonder what Lew will owe him after this?" said Ray as he pulled on the gloves. The driver's side door of the van was unlocked and opened easily. The seat around the van's owner was blood-soaked, even though the front of the T-shirt was unmarked.

"Hmm, doesn't look good," said Ray. He gave the dead man's shoulder a gentle shove. The body fell forward onto the steering wheel. White as the front of the T-shirt might be, the back was blood-black. Working his gloved fingers gingerly, Osborne was able to lift the shirt high enough to see the source of Mike Kelly's deep slumber: a single knife wound under the left shoulder blade.

While Ray moved back from the van to uncap the lens on his camera, Osborne checked his phone for cell service. He had two bars, enough to alert Lew, who answered after two rings.

"Check for the fifty thousand in cash," she said. "The girlfriend said he was carrying it in a money belt under his shirt."

"No sign of a money belt," said Osborne. "Just so you know, whoever did this must have left on foot. Ray can tell that only one vehicle drove in here. Right now the ground in this clearing is still soft enough that he is photographing any footprints that don't belong to us. Hold on a moment, Lew . . ." Osborne held his phone away as he called to Ray, "Any sign of a vehicle driving out of here?"

"No. But I see at least two deer trails leading in the direction of the Ericsson property. Tell Lew that I'll double-check the plat book, but I believe the Ericsson property line is located beyond the stream running behind this berm. Tell her that it makes sense to me to start my ground search here."

"What about the guy's phone?" was Lew's next question. "If you can find that, we can check his messages and texts—"

"Hold on," said Osborne. After scanning the bloody seat of the van he pushed aside an empty McDonald's bag on the floor, but found nothing. He reached a gloved hand down into the opening between the passenger and driver's seats. "No phone that I can see. Lew and I don't want to disturb the contents of this van until Bruce can check it out. I assume you'll have him work up this site, too?"

"Hell on the budget, but I'll have to. Do you mind holding the line? I'm going to check with the phone company and see if that cell signal is still alive."

Osborne waited until Lew came back on. "Doc, it's around there somewhere. I'm going to e-mail you a GPS setting from the phone tech. I'll bet it got tossed in the woods back there."

Ray, standing nearby, walked over and pulled his own phone from his back pocket. "I have an idea, Doc. Ask Chief Ferris what kind of phone the guy had. And if it's an iPhone, see if the girl-friend has his Apple ID—it's what he would use to order off iTunes."

"Lew, did you hear that?" asked Osborne.

"I did. Hold the line and I'll see if I can reach her ... okay, here it is."

"Hold on, now," said Ray, as he punched Mike Kelly's ID into his own phone, "I have an app called Find My Phone that just might help us ... yep, there it is." He held up his phone, and Osborne could see a small gray phone icon that the phone was quite close to the van. "Tell Chief Ferris, it's so close that I'll find it within a few minutes, I'm sure."

"Call me ASAP when you do," said Lew. "I know it's getting late, Doc, but will you and Ray please stay there until I can get Todd or Roger out to close off the entrance?"

"Of course, but don't worry too much. It's tough to see from the road. I don't think this place gets a lot of visitors."

Osborne waited while Ray crossed the clearing in the direction of the stream, which they could hear gurgling just beyond the berm. Pulling a pair of polarized sunglasses from his shirt pocket, he waded into the stream, his eyes moving back and forth between the icon on his phone and his feet.

"Score," he said, leaning over to stare down into the shallow streambed. "Doc, better hand me another pair of gloves—we got a soggy cell phone here."

An hour later, standing in Jane Ericsson's driveway with Lew, Osborne, and Ray, Bruce pursed his lips and wrinkled his brows as he studied the wet cell phone. Its battery had run down so there was no longer even a signal. "Too bad," said Bruce, "who knows what we might have found on this besides the fact that someone wiped all the prints off it. I'll send it down to the lab but it may be a lost cause. I dropped my iPhone in the toilet last month and our tech couldn't get that to work."

"All ... is not lost," said Ray, raising the index finger of his right hand. "I have rice at my place. Want me to give it a try?"

"You talking some kind of witchcraft?" asked Bruce with a sneer. He pushed his glasses up his nose and blinked at Ray.

"Not ... at all. Believe it or not," said Ray with one of his pauses that indicated he was about to deliver information that would change the lives of everyone nearby, "rice works. Tried it myself a couple months ago when I dropped my Android off the dock. Uncooked rice is a powerful absorbent. All I had to do was submerge my phone and the battery in a bowl of dry rice for twenty-four hours and it worked fine ... well, kinda fine. I lost my birdcall ringtone, but otherwise the phone works great."

"Did you have voicemails on it, and were you able to get those?" asked Lew.

"Yep. I was expecting a call from a client from Chicago, and it came through clear as a bell. Otherwise I would've lost a good guiding gig. Let me take care of it, okay?"

Lew looked hesitant. "Chief," said Ray, "it'll cost you two bucks ... for the rice."

She glanced over at Bruce, who shrugged and said, "Worth a try. I know my tech can't do it."

Chapter Eighteen

It was six o'clock when they all gathered in Lew's office at the police station. Ray laid Mike Kelly's cell phone on the round table in the corner that Lew used for meetings. He had slipped it into a Ziploc bag, which was slightly fogged from the water that kept dripping from the phone.

"I'm not sure I'm with you on this rice thing," said Bruce, who had been pushing the bag around. "Not sure at all."

"You got something better, you take it," said Ray. "All I can say is that rice worked on my phone." He pulled his cell phone from his shirt pocket and handed it to Bruce. "See what you think."

Bruce shook his head as he said, "Okay, let me see if I can get any prints off this first. Then you give it a try. If that doesn't work, we'll send it to the phone company and see what they can do."

Lew, leaning back against her desk with her arms folded, said, "I'm okay with this. If I have a working phone with the victim's recent messages by late tomorrow, it's worth a try. We know the phone company said it will take them days to resurrect it, and even then they can't promise it'll work."

The door to the office opened and Mallory entered, followed by Kenton. "Mind if Kenton sits in on our conference?" she asked. "He has some new info on one of the senior people on Jane Ericsson's campaign staff."

"Really," said Lew. "Kenton, I don't recall asking you to join the investigation. If you've been going around questioning people—"

"Gosh, no," said Kenton. "I just—overheard something, that's all."

Lew hesitated before saying, "Well . . . okay, but everyone here has been working since early, early this morning. I'm only interested in facts right now, Kenton. Not hearsay. But you go ahead, sit over there by Dani. Just keep what you hear in confidence. Understand?" Kenton nodded in agreement.

Osborne turned away so no one would see him grin. He suspected she had agreed to let him stay to accommodate Mallory.

"If there is anything I don't need it's someone like you jeopardizing the integrity of this investigation. The only people who should be in here right now are Doc, Ray, Bruce, Dani, and Mallory. Mallory because she's helping me handle the press, and my tech, Dani, because she's taking notes and handling our online research."

Dani, a chubby brunette who was sitting back in one corner, waved a hand at the crew. Lew had brought her on board a year ago after the cosmetology major at the local tech college had turned out to be a wizard at using computer databases for investigative searches.

"I understand," said Kenton. He opened his mouth to say more when Lew said, "Whatever you've got to say—later. I need to hear from the crime lab first. Bruce, you start."

"Thanks, Chief. I've examined what we have of the victim, Jane Ericsson." Bruce looked down at his notes. "What we have is the head, the right leg, the left forearm, one foot and two sections of the torso—six body parts total. Bert Gilligan's crews have crawled through the storm sewer where it is wide enough, and found nothing. They have also been diligent in watching the surface water where it flows into the culvert on Woodland Avenue, as well as the culvert that empties into the Tomorrow River. So far, nothing there, either.

"However, the severing of the body parts was so skillful, the knives used so sharp, that I am convinced we're looking for someone who is a butcher—or was a butcher. This person is more skilled than a surgeon. One thing we still have to test for, even though it seems obvious, is to confirm the DNA of all the body parts—that they are all from the same individual.

"My youngest sister is a research doc in pediatrics, working down in Kansas City, and she is at a hospital with a pediatric genome lab that has perfected a speedy sequencing of DNA for treating babies. Our goal is simpler: we are just trying to match the DNA samples from each body part. I sent the samples down to my sister late today, and she thinks she may be able to confirm a match some time tomorrow, or early Tuesday at the latest."

"I have one problem with your theory that we're looking for a butcher," said Ray. "Lots of people around here butcher their deer. Lots. I mean, everyone hunts, and no one likes paying to have their meat butchered."

"I know that," said Bruce. "But this person is better than an amateur who cuts up a deer once a year. We're looking for an experienced butcher. And it was someone who had access to Jane Ericsson's house." Bruce let his statement hang in the air.

Osborne dropped his head so no one could see the worry in his eyes. Should he mention that Kaye Lund was one of the best butchers of deer in the region? The fact that she and Jane had recently fallen out? That Kaye lived so close? That grim thought was countered by his memory of Kaye's difficulty moving—it was hard for her to get out of her rocking chair, even. He decided not to say anything . . . yet.

"What makes you think so?" asked Lew.

"On a hunch early this afternoon, I pulled the drains in the kitchen at the Ericsson place—the sink against the wall on your right when you enter from the stairs leading up from the driveway, and the sink in that kitchen island. I found what I am sure is human blood in both." Before anyone could open their mouths, Bruce grinned. "Yep, it's been sent off with the tissue samples to my sister for DNA analysis.

"Once I found that, I closed off the kitchen from the living room so I had low light, and sprayed the entire kitchen with luminol. I found trace amounts of blood on the cutting board surfaces on the island, as well as where it had dripped down the cabinet fronts and onto the floor. Also traces on the counters beside the sink. Someone did a very nice job of cleaning up, but not nice enough. And it sure as hell isn't deer season."

Lew heaved a sigh of relief. "Thanks, Bruce. Good progress on that front. Doc, what do you know about the victim in the van?"

Osborne sat up in his chair. "I talked to Mike Kelly's girlfriend two hours ago. She is driving up from Madison to the Wausau Crime Lab where she will ID the body in the morning. Bruce is still working with the van and the victim, right?"

Osborne looked over at Bruce who said, "Yes, I'm having the body driven down to Wausau shortly. I want to be sure we have all trace evidence cataloged before letting it go. But, Doc, you had interesting observations—tell Chief Ferris what you found."

"Not being a pathologist, I do the best I can," said Osborne. "Once Bruce got to the van to help me so we could be sure not to damage the wound track, I slipped my palms under the victim's arms. I would have felt some warmth if he hadn't been dead long, but the body was cold and clammy, which makes me think he died eighteen to twenty-four hours ago. Rigor mortis speeds up in heat like this, so that was no help. Since the victim had lost a lot of blood through his wound, we didn't see significant lividity, either. Some putrefaction was setting in—"

"I'll say," said Ray. "You did not want to get too close to that poor sucker."

"And no money?"

"No money."

"Well," said Lew, sitting back in her chair, "a lot accomplished, but no lead on our killer." She looked across the room to where Mallory sat listening. "What do we say to the press now?"

"Nothing, unless we have the local TV crew out there. Shortly after noon today, a major sex scandal broke in Washington, D.C. They're gone."

"You're kidding."

"No, you can relax. For the local media, I suggest you wait until tomorrow morning and we'll give them something then, around ten A.M. or so. If you'd like, Chief Ferris, I'll work on a press release tonight and show it to you tomorrow for any changes you want. Then Dani and I will hand some out, and e-mail the rest. The media horde may be gone," she said with a chuckle, "but Dani and I have about fifty business cards."

"Okay, folks, if that's it," said Lew, getting to her feet.

"Wait! What about me?" asked Kenton. "My information could be a turning point in this case."

Lew sat back down. "The floor is yours, Kenton."

"So this morning after Ray left Mallory and me with his friend, Christina, we were standing out in the driveway by the Ericsson place—you know, when you stepped outside and Lauren Crowell came out with you?"

"I remember," said Lew.

"Well, Christina recognized her." Kenton stepped into the middle of the room and made eye contact with everyone as he spoke. "She said that one of the assistants in the art gallery up in Manitowish Waters had caught Lauren stealing hair extensions worth hundreds of dollars."

The room was silent. Lew's voice was gentle as she said, "Kenton, there is an old saying in law enforcement: The worst witness is an eyewitness."

"You don't believe me?" Kenton looked flustered.

"I believe you. I don't believe Christina what's-her-name's assistant, or even Christina herself. Do they have this on a surveillance tape?"

"I asked about that, but they recycle their videotape every forty-eight hours, so no."

"Thank you for trying, Kenton."

Osborne watched as a deep red flooded into the young man's face. "One more thing, Chief Ferris—"

"Can you keep it short?" asked Lew. "We're all ready to leave."

"I asked one of the campaign staffers where Lauren Crowell lives—you know, where her home is, where she used to work—stuff everyone knows about me, or about Mallory. And *no one knows anything.*"

"Kenton, it's obvious you have it out for the woman. I think you'd better tone it down."

Kenton closed his eyes as he said, "Chief Ferris, trust me, I just know something is not right about her. Is there any reason not to run a background check on her? A criminal background check—not just a Google search." He glanced over at Dani. "I can help Dani. I'll bet we could do it in fifteen minutes."

Lew mulled over his request. "On one condition, Kenton. Get the names of all the staff working in the local office. I would be more comfortable if we can say we're running background checks on the whole crew. Plus, I have to admit it makes sense.

"Now, it is after six, people. Go home and get some rest. Bruce, can you finish up pretty soon? You and Doc have been up as long as I have."

"No fishing tonight?" asked Bruce.

Lew gave him the dim eye. Delighted with his own cleverness, Bruce's eyebrows jumped around. With that, they all got to their feet to file out of the office. Lew was the last one out, and she locked the door behind them.

Chapter Nineteen

Lew poured herself an iced tea, and walked down through the field behind her little farmhouse to the wooden swing that looked out over the pond. The sun had dropped behind the tall pines on the peninsula to her right, cooling the night air. Bats had begun to swoop in the shadows, hungry for the mosquitoes that were just waking up.

With the creaking of the swing, her shoulders relaxed. The lemon in the tea soothed her throat. So much talking today—questions from the reporters, the mayor, everyone on staff needing direction. She was tired but satisfied. And tonight, her own bed. A firefly grazed her knee.

She remembered how her grandfather had let her sleep outside on nights just like this: the breezes soft, the distant wailing of a loon. Lew smiled to herself. Ever since getting to know Ray Pradt and his encyclopedia of birdcalls, she didn't trust herself to judge if it was a real bird or Ray putting her on.

Tonight it was a real loon. That she was sure of, since everyone from Ray to Doc to Bruce had to feel as bone tired as she did.

Taking a final swallow of tea, she sensed someone approaching. She turned to look over her right shoulder. A curtain of dusk had fallen across the field behind her. It was empty. She turned back to the lake, her body tensing. She could feel it in her back: someone was watching. She turned around fast. No one.

Then, in her peripheral vision to the left, she saw a dark shadow move along the fence surrounding the apple orchard. But the moment she saw it, it was gone—vanished into the woods. Had she really seen something? Someone?

Lew got to her feet and kidded herself for feeling so vulnerable. She knew the local wolf pack had grown in numbers, and the young were scouting new territory. That must have been what she saw. Nothing to be afraid of; just a wolf.

After setting down his copy of *Trout Madness*, which he was rereading for the umpteenth time, Osborne turned out the light on his bedside table. The windows were open to the moonlight; a breeze off the lake cooled his forehead. He was missing one thing: Lewellyn. He slept better when she was beside him.

A soft knock on the bedroom door brought him up on one elbow. "Dad?"

Osborne sat up and swung his legs over the side of the bed. "Just a second, Mal, hon." He pulled on his bathrobe and opened the door.

"Can we talk for a minute? I know it's late, but—"

"No, this is fine. Where's Kenton? Want to go out on the porch? Cooler out there."

"No, Dad. I don't want Kenton to hear me." She dropped her head, and in the pale glow from the moon, he thought he saw tears in her eyes.

"Dad, what do you think of him—of Kenton, I mean?"

That was a tough one. Osborne hesitated. He had made so many mistakes with this daughter, and only in the last two years had they seemed to find the closeness that had been missing since she was a child. He had to be very careful.

"I guess," said Osborne, "my question is . . . is there room for you in his life? He's always on the phone or on his computer. I'm not sure he hears you when you're talking to him. I know Kenton has a big job, but he's just so busy."

"You think he's a jerk."

"Narcissist is a kinder word. It's all about him, sweetie. The phone calls, the e-mails, the schedule the way he wants it, the likes, the dislikes. I could see he was irritated that Lew asked you—not him—to take charge of the media today."

"Was Mom like that? Always having to be in control?"

"That's how I know one when I see one. Experience counts."

Mallory was silent for so long that Osborne wondered if he had just said the wrong thing. She had been her mother's favorite for so many years. To the exclusion of Osborne himself, which he hadn't realized and accepted until he was in therapy during his rehab at Hazelden.

"Kenton's a lot like my ex, isn't he?"

"Your mother liked your first husband. I didn't. I'm afraid I told you that at the wrong time."

"Yeah, the night before my wedding. Thanks, Dad." He could see a rueful smile cross her face.

"I am so sorry. Am I doing it again?"

"Heavens, no." She waved a dismissive hand. "This way I have time to make a change." She smiled. "And it is a lot less expensive this way. I think, actually I know, that Mom would have liked Kenton."

"I am sure she would. He's good-looking, he has the impressive title, and he will make a lot of money. But, Mallory, do you want to be right? Or do you want to be loved?"

"Dad," she said, "I want what you and Lew have—you have fun together, you have a great friendship, such an *appreciation* of each other. What's the secret, Dad? How do I find that?"

"Take fly fishing lessons?"

Mallory laughed. "You're right. No easy answer."

"Sorry if I'm hard on Kenton, but you asked my opinion."

"Yes, I did."

"And you wanted an honest answer?"

"I did. I guess the problem is me. I'm just not sure any more if I'm any good at judging people."

Osborne said nothing. He couldn't help her there. He was the one who had spent over thirty years married to a woman who grimaced at the sound of his voice.

"Good night, and thanks, Dad." Mallory stood up, gave him a peck on the cheek, and opened the bedroom door.

"Good night, sweetheart . . . I love you."

Too late; she was out the door, and hadn't heard him.

The next morning after breakfast, while his guests took the dog for a walk, Osborne went downstairs to be sure there was enough toilet tissue in the bathroom that Kenton and Mallory were using. Both bedrooms were in use: Mallory had moved out of the one she had been sharing with Kenton.

Chapter Twenty

Osborne left the house early Monday on a hunch that Lew would be at her desk before seven. He was right. Not only was she was there, but the coffee pot was half empty.

"I thought I would finish my paperwork on the victim recovery yesterday," he said, walking into her office. Lew glanced up. "Want me to work here," he pointed to a chair in the corner behind the table, "or in the conference room?"

"In here, if the phone and the scanner don't bother you, Doc. I just left a message over at the Inn for Lauren Crowell. I want to meet with her first thing this morning—"

As she was speaking, the phone rang. Lew picked up. "Yes, Marlaine, that's fine. Put her through." Lew signaled with her eyes that it was Lauren. "Morning, Lauren. Say, we had a development late yesterday that Dr. Osborne and I would like to discuss with you. How soon can you meet with us here in my office? Yes, the Loon Lake police located right behind the courthouse. The front desk will be expecting you. Thank you, Lauren."

"What's new since last night?" asked Osborne.

"Nothing yet. We're waiting on the results of the samples that Bruce sent down south, and Ray will be spending today scouring the Ericsson property. In the meantime, I want to get a handle on anyone who may have been in that house Friday night."

Lauren arrived within half an hour. "Sorry if I look bad," she said as she took a chair beside Osborne in front of Lew's desk. In fact, thought Osborne, she looked rested and relaxed. Maybe she thought she *should* look bad.

"Lauren," said Lew, "a thorough investigation of Jane Ericsson's house indicates that she died there sometime during the night Friday. We're hoping you can tell us the names of any people—workmen included—who may have been in or around Jane's house during the day or later that evening."

"Let me think about this for a minute," said Lauren, concentration wrinkling her forehead. "Well … you have me down in Madison, though I was in the house until around noon Friday before leaving to drive down. I don't remember seeing any workmen around, though that doesn't mean they didn't come by later."

"We've learned that Jane had plans to meet with a Mike Kelly that evening. Does his name mean anything to you?"

"Oh, that guy. He was a pest. He showed up at almost every rally. But Jane was due home so late that it doesn't make sense she would have made an appointment to see him. I suggest you ask him about that—if you can find him."

"What do you mean, 'if we can find him'?" asked Osborne.

"He lives in his van, I think. I can't imagine that he can be reached very easily—except by phone, of course. I can assure you, no one on staff has his number. We tried to ignore the guy. Like I said, he was a pest. And a nut case, in my opinion."

"Anyone else, Lauren?" asked Lew.

The woman gave a heavy sigh and said, "Well, of course, that old frog next door might have tried something. She used to come in and out all the time, without knocking. Even though Jane tried to put an end to that, she may have found a way to get in."

"You're referring to Kaye Lund, I assume?" asked Osborne, his voice stern as a parent. Lauren's snarky comments about Kaye were wearing on him.

"Were locks changed recently?" asked Lew.

"Yes. But that didn't help. Jane often left her doors unlocked—especially when she was drinking. I got so mad at her for that."

"I'm sorry," said Lew, "I think I asked you this before and forgot to write it down, but who did you say you had planned to stay with in Madison? Before you got the news about Jane."

"Phyllis Cook. She's a good friend who always has a spare bunk for me."

"Would Jane have stayed there, too?"

"Heavens, no. She was to stay with the Winters at their home in Maple Grove. They were hosting the event on the pontoon. That's why I wanted her to fly into Madison instead of spending the night up here. If only she had taken my advice, but no, she insisted on staying here Friday; said she was exhausted. May I ask what makes you so sure that Jane was . . . that she died in her home?"

"Sorry," said Lew, "that's confidential until I have all the results in. Doc, do you have any more questions for Lauren?"

"Will you be at the memorial service tomorrow?" asked Osborne. "Kaye told me it was scheduled for ten A.M."

A wave of irritation crossed Lauren's face before she answered. "Of course. I'm giving the campaign staff their final notices later today, so I'm sure many of them will be there, too." Lauren stood up. "I have one thought, by the way. Our campaign got so much attention all these months that someone I never knew or saw might have targeted Jane. She was in the public eye so often, who knows what deranged person might have decided to . . ."

"Good point," said Lew. "I'll be in touch when we can allow you back in the house for the rest of your things."

Early that afternoon, Bruce poked his head around Lew's door. "Chief Ferris, got a minute? Just had an e-mail from my sister at the pediatric genome lab—the DNA samples all match. We have one victim. Just one."

"What about the blood samples that you found at the Ericsson house?"

"The DNA in the blood is a match to the other samples. No question in my mind that that is where the Ericsson woman was killed and her body dismembered."

"Have we heard anything from Ray yet?"

"Nothing new. He has laid out a grid pattern with ropes to be sure he works the entire area. Told me he's hoping to finish before dark."

"Well, you two," said Lew, rocking back in her chair. "Looks like we're stalled for a while."

"Kenton texted me a few minutes ago asking if Dani has run the background check on Lauren Crowell yet," said Osborne.

"Oh, right," said Lew, sitting up fast. "My mistake—I forgot to tell her to run Crowell's name along with all the local staffers through the NCIC. Someone broke into the pharmacy across from the sports bar during the storm Friday night, and she has been up to her ears trying to find current addresses for our local meth abusers. I'll have her run that check as soon as she's done with the other."

Bruce checked his watch and said, "Say, guys, I don't expect the pathology report on the victim found in the van for awhile. How about a couple hours in the trout stream?"

Lew's face brightened then fell. "I can't fit all three of us in my pickup."

"I'll drive," said Osborne. "Bruce, did you bring your fly rod?"

"You must be kidding," said Bruce with a pleased chortle.

In the thirty minutes it took Osborne to drive out to his place, change clothes, pack his fishing gear into the back of his Subaru, and drive back to the police department, Lew had changed out of her uniform and into dark green fishing shorts, a tan T-shirt, and her fly fishing vest. She and Bruce, also dressed for action in the water, were sitting on the stoop at the back door to the station as Osborne pulled up. After stowing their gear in the back, they scrambled into the car.

"Got waders?" Osborne turned sideways to ask Bruce. He didn't have to ask Lew. She drove her pickup in to the department every morning, except in the dead of winter, with her gear (which included a half-inflated float tube and a bike pump) at the ready for fishing on a moment's notice.

When Osborne kidded her for never leaving home without a fly rod, she would laugh and say, "Hey, when you live this close to water, you never know when you can snatch half an hour here or an hour there. No better way to take your mind off a day's problems and let the old subconscious work."

An excellent excuse, and maybe even true, thought Osborne. After all, he liked to say he practiced dentistry so he could afford to fish.

"Yep, got waders, got a couple new dry flies, and a box of #16 Adams that I tied myself," said Bruce, slouching happily in the back seat.

"We're heading for my favorite stream north of here," said Lew to Bruce. "It's less than an hour away, in case something breaks on the investigation and we have to get back fast. But it's also secret water that few people know about."

"What stream is it?" asked Bruce.

"Secret Stream," said Lew.

"Oh, all right, I get the message," said Bruce with a pout. "It's still so warm—do you think we'll see any brookies?"

"Depends if there's a hatch or not. This time of year, that's iffy. The rain should have cooled the water down, but you never know. It is August, after all."

Following Lew's instructions, Osborne pulled off the highway and down an unmarked country lane before parking alongside some farmer's fence. Moving quickly, they piled out of the car and grabbed their gear.

Ten minutes before Osborne and Bruce had finished threading their fly lines and tying on new leaders, Lew was ready: waders belted, fly rod in her right hand, polarized sunglasses perched on the curls crowding her forehead, and two boxes of trout flies tucked into her shirt pockets. She waited patiently before leading them down a narrow path to enter the water near a beaver dam that had been pulled apart by earlier visitors.

"This is when I love life," said Bruce as he splashed into the stream. Osborne agreed. The afternoon sun was hot on their shoulders, but a steady breeze eased the heat. The water in the stream was running fast and clear, burbling around large boulders and spilling over shelves of rock and stone left by the glacier as it had carved its way through the Northwoods.

"No hatch," said Lew with a shrug. "Doesn't mean it isn't dinnertime somewhere." She smiled. Hatch or no hatch, she was happy.

After forging upstream forty feet, Bruce made his first cast. "Oh, dear," said Lew. "Do that again." Bruce raised his right arm to send the fly line up, back, and forward where, instead of unfurling thirty to forty feet ahead . . . it puddled at his feet.

"Too much wrist," said Lew. "I didn't teach you that. And, Bruce, your back cast sucks—you got loops, when that line should flow straight back on a nice, level plane. And your stance . . . honestly, Bruce, you have picked up some bad habits. Watch me," she said, "try to be more fluid in your movement. Even Doc back casts better than you."

"Thanks," said Osborne drily, though he was tickled with the backhanded compliment.

Lew waded into the middle of the stream to demonstrate. With her right arm at her side, she set her right foot slightly behind as she held her fly rod at a forty-five-degree angle, then turned her hips and shoulders, keeping her elbow firm and not elevated. The fly line whipped back and forth on a level plane until she stopped the rod abruptly, letting the fly line unfurl nearly sixty feet and drop her dry fly with such delicacy, there was not even a whisper as it landed.

"You got a better rod than I do," said Bruce, sputtering. "You got that Joan Wulff-designed rod with the thumb groove."

"No excuses, Bruce," said Lew. "You can make a good cast no matter what rod you've got. Remember the three rules I taught you—or tried to teach you. One: if you're right-handed, your right foot should be positioned to the rear. Bruce, that's the first thing you forgot. Two: be sure your casting-hand thumb is positioned behind the rod handle. And three: *do not raise your elbow on the cast.* I know it's counterintuitive, but think of keeping your elbow on a shelf that's as high as your elbow—*no higher.* Okay, try again. This time, watch that wrist!"

Bruce tried, and tried . . . and tried. After half an hour, while Osborne busied himself casting further upstream, Lew finally said, "Better. You're still letting that rod tip drift up too high, but it's coming." She sighed. "You will catch fish, Bruce, but you've still got a lot to learn. I want to see your casting improve.

"You, too, Doc," she said, loud enough for Osborne to hear. "I want to see that back cast of yours parallel to the ground. All right, you two, I'm heading upstream. See you later."

Each in their own world, they fished until dark. As the full moon rose through the feathery fingers of tamarack growing in the bogs along the rushing water, Osborne found himself in a section where the stream narrowed to less than ten feet wide. A patch of brush on one side held ripening wild raspberries. Even as he relished the thought of a luscious berry or two, he realized they would have more appeal to another denizen of the woods: a bear. Maybe a young bear. Maybe a young bear followed by a hungry wolf. Osborne knew he was letting his imagination get the better of him, but he was also hungry, and not a little fatigued.

At the sound of splashing, he caught his breath. But it was only Lew coming toward him, Bruce a shadow behind her. "Doc, have you had enough? It's getting late. I'm afraid I lost track of time. Neither Bruce nor I had even a rise. What about you?"

"Nope, but no complaints. A beautiful night in the water." He decided against mentioning his imaginary but worrisome bear and wolf.

After they packed up their gear and climbed back into the Subaru, Bruce said, "I've been thinking about that Lauren woman and your son-in-law's comment that she may have been seen shoplifting—"

"He's not my son-in-law," said Osborne, interrupting. "Not yet anyway. Hopefully not ever."

Lew gave Osborne a funny look. "Don't hold back, Doc."

"I don't like the guy. He's a bully. Anyway, Lew seemed to think that Christina, Ray's friend who mentioned the shoplifting incident, was likely mistaken."

"That may be," said Bruce. "But I heard Kenton telling Dani that people tell you who they are, who they *really* are, in unexpected ways: comments, gestures. That's what I like about my work at the crime lab: I keep an eye out for the little stuff, the off-kilter detail that gives it all away. I'm always learning, and I like that."

Lew turned to look back at Bruce. "Okay, then, student—if you're so smart, what are the four phases of fishing?"

Glancing up at his rearview mirror, Osborne saw Bruce grinning as he said in a singsong voice, "I know. Phase One is when you want to *catch* a fish. Phase Two is when you want to catch a *lot* of fish. Phase Three is when you want to catch a *big* fish. And Phase Four is . . ."

At that they all chimed in together: " . . . *when you just want to be able to fish.*"

Checking with the switchboard for messages as Osborne drove through the dark, Lew learned that Ray had found nothing to indicate anyone had been trespassing on the Ericsson property. Even the workmen had come and gone in predictable ways.

Osborne had a message from Mallory that she and Kenton had gone to a movie, but she had made a cold macaroni salad that she knew was one of Osborne's favorites, and it was waiting for him in the fridge. "And, Dad, I left four ears of corn from the farmers' market along with two fresh tomatoes on the kitchen counter."

Bruce checked his messages and heard that the pathology report on Mike Kelly was waiting for him on his computer back at his room at the Loon Lake Inn. Anxious to see it, he made Osborne drop him off first.

After Bruce had gathered up his fishing gear and headed off, Osborne turned to Lew. "Dinner at my place?" She smiled a response. And the evening was swell.

Chapter Twenty-One

By nine-fifteen the next morning, St. Mary's Church was half full. By ten, the church was packed and people were shoulder to shoulder in the vestibule. Following the celebration of the Mass, Kaye walked up to the podium. She pulled the mike toward her and started to speak, but choked. She tried again, but couldn't get a word out. Shaking her head, she turned to start back toward her seat. Ray, who had been sitting beside her in the pew, rushed up to take her by the arm and guide her.

Meanwhile, Father John stepped up to the mic and introduced a young woman, one of the college students who had been staffing the Loon Lake campaign office. The student spoke to Jane's skills as a candidate and the student's conviction that she would have won the race.

Next was an old friend and colleague of Jane's who had flown in from Washington, D.C., that morning after hearing news of Jane's death on television. She talked of how Jane's law career had been outstanding and that she, too, knew that Jane would have made a fine senator.

Finally, there were a few words from Father John as he invited everyone in the church to the parish hall for an early lunch.

"No mention was made of the circumstances of her death," Osborne heard one television reporter say as he was taped standing on the stairs outside the church. Osborne ducked his head and hurried by. Earlier that morning, Mallory had warned Osborne and Lew to expect some reporters hoping for updates on the investigation. That was enough for Lew. She had decided not to attend the service.

As he walked into the parish hall cafeteria, Osborne spotted Kaye sitting with Mallory, Ray, and Kenton. He joined them as they lined up to file past the ladies serving up plates of fried chicken, mashed potatoes and gravy, green beans, and slices of blueberry pie. They walked back to their table and started to eat.

As people continued to file in and find seats at the long tables, Osborne saw Lauren Crowell enter the room, look around, and choose a seat to herself off in the farthest corner. She laid her purse on the table but made no move to get food. Osborne decided to keep an eye on her as she watched the room. *Be interesting to see who she might talk to.*

Within ten minutes the cafeteria was nearly full, though the chair opposite Osborne was empty until Bob Kuhl, who had been in Mallory's high school class, sat down with a heaping plate of food.

"Hey, Mallory," he said. "I haven't seen you in years. What are you up to?"

"Got myself an MBA and I'm working in marketing down in Chicago," said Mallory. "How about you?"

"I'm an accountant in my dad's firm," said Bob. "We handle the bookkeeping for the Ericsson estate and for Jane Ericsson's campaign."

"A lot of money invested in that campaign, I hear," said Kenton, who was sitting beside Osborne.

"You would be surprised how much—over a million, and that's not counting what Jane herself put in," said Bob before tucking into the heap of potatoes in front of him. He ate with such relish that Osborne wondered when he had had his last meal. With one chicken wing remaining, Bob exhaled, wiped at his mouth, and said, "Dr. Osborne, I hear you're working part-time for Chief Ferris these days? You helping with the Ericsson murder investigation?"

"Up to a point," said Osborne, reluctant to say more. "I'm more helpful to Chief Ferris when a dental ID is needed, or when Pecore, our coroner, is not available. Right now he's in Madison on business, so I was called in help out, but only on the basics. I'm no medical examiner—but how did you know?"

"Our firm does the payroll for the town, so I see your checks every once in a while." Bob gnawed on the chicken wing, then pushed his chair back, reached for his plate, and stood up. "Say, Dr. Osborne, I'd like to have a minute with you if I could."

"In private?" Osborne was taken aback.

"Well, how 'bout the hallway? I just don't want to be shouting, y'know."

"Sure. Kenton, Mallory, would you excuse me, please?" asked Osborne as he got up to follow Bob out of the cafeteria. They walked down the hall to a cloakroom and Bob closed the door behind them.

"Doc, it may be nothing, but I'm concerned over something that's been happening with the campaign accounts, and I would appreciate it if you would mention it to Chief Ferris. Starting ten days ago, someone has been withdrawing large sums of money using Jane Ericsson's access codes and password. We're talking fifty to a hundred thousand at a shot, but no record of who, what, and why. My job is to keep on top of those records so the campaign isn't hit with legal issues.

"What really worries me is that I spoke with Jane on the phone last Monday, and she had no idea this was happening and why. She planned to talk it over with her staff and get back to me, but she never did. But here's the strangest thing: someone pulled a hundred thousand dollars out of the account just this morning, *using Jane Ericsson's access code and password.*"

Osborne stared at him. "Using Jane Ericsson's personal information?"

"Right. I thought you might want to let Chief Ferris know. I'll be in the office all afternoon if she wants to check with me."

"Back up for a minute," said Osborne. "Was this happening this way before? I'm surprised Jane would be taking money from the campaign."

"That's what caught my eye," said Bob. "It's unusual. Each campaign office has a person designated to handle expenses. They contact me, submit invoices, and I e-mail the funds into the accounts. Jane, of course, has had access from the beginning, but never used it until ten days ago. She did it via her cell phone, if that helps. It didn't occur to me until just before the memorial service this morning—when I stopped by the office and saw that last transaction—that someone may have stolen her cell phone."

"But that wouldn't work unless they had her password, right?"

"It puzzles me, Doc. I wanted to share this without anyone hearing. God forbid the wrong person be accused."

"Who would that be?"

"Well . . ." Bob hesitated. "For a couple years now, Jane was the co-signer on a credit card that Kaye Lund used. But that has always been small stuff like groceries, meds—nothing like this."

"Correct me if I'm wrong," said Osborne, "but the funds that worry you have all been withdrawn from the campaign account, not Jane's personal account?"

"Right. But that may be because anything over ten thousand dollars must be approved by the executor of the Ericsson estate—and that's one of the senior executives at the bank that manages the estate's investments. You can't get those funds as quickly as the campaign funds, because no one has set an official limit on campaign-related withdrawals."

Kenton and Mallory were waiting in the hall when Osborne and Bob came out of the cloakroom. "What was that all about? asked Kenton.

"Oh, Bob has some personal concerns he wanted to discuss," said Osborne. Kenton was getting on his nerves. He had to make an effort not to ask Mallory how soon she might drive the guy back to Chicago.

"Dr. Osborne," said Bob as they walked toward the door, "I see Chuck Winters over in the corner. He was one of the largest donors to Jane's campaign, and he flew up from Madison this morning. Do you mind if I introduce you? I think he would appreciate some feedback on the investigation—if you don't mind."

"I'm happy to say hello to the man," said Osborne, "but I'm afraid I have nothing to say on the investigation. He'll have to touch base with Chief Ferris on that."

Before he could say more, Winters had walked over to put an arm over Bob's shoulder. "Bob, you holding up okay? I know you worked closely with Jane."

"Doing all right, Chuck, thanks for asking." With a nod toward Osborne, Bob said, "Chuck, I'd like you to meet one of the forensic experts working on the case."

Osborne extended his right hand to shake Winter's as he said, "That's a bit of an overstatement, I'm afraid. I'm retired from a dental practice, but I cover the odontology needed by the Wausau Crime Lab and the Loon Lake Police. Afraid I'm not well versed enough to give you any information on the investigation at the moment."

"It is a devastating turn of events," said Winters. "I had so much faith in what Jane could do for Wisconsin. I knew her father."

"So did I," said Osborne. "I understand you were planning to host a gathering of supporters the other evening?"

"Yes. We were having cocktails on the pontoon when I tried to reach her and see what was holding her up, but her phone just rang and rang."

"Do you recall what time you made the first call?" asked Osborne, realizing this might give Bruce and Lew a better handle on just when Jane had become unreachable. "I know Lauren Crowell said she was trying her as of eight o'clock or so."

"Lauren who?" asked Winters.

"Her campaign manager. I believe she was one of the organizers of your event. A tall, black-haired woman? Slender, attractive." Osborne glanced around to see if Lauren might be in the vicinity.

"Um, no, we worked with the Madison-based staff. Not sure who you're talking about."

"Lauren Crowell," Osborne repeated. "She told the investigating team that she was on your boat Friday night, waiting for Jane to show up."

"We were only twelve people, Dr. Osborne. I knew everyone there. My wife and I invited everyone personally. I don't believe I've even heard the name, but whoever she is—she was not in our home Friday night." Winters handed Osborne a business card and said, "Please call if I can help in any way. My wife and I are beside ourselves—still can't believe it."

Osborne hurried toward the parking lot, anxious to get over to Lew's office. "Doc, wait," said Kenton as he ran toward Osborne with Mallory close behind. He stopped suddenly at one of the cars just pulling out of the lot: a black Jeep.

Kenton stepped out in front of the Jeep, forcing Lauren to a stop. She opened her window to demand, "What—"

"Just a quick word is all," Osborne heard Kenton say in a friendly tone. "Tell me the name of your company again? I was trying to look you up on LinkedIn, but I must have misspelled the name. I want to stay in touch in case our firm can submit some proposals—"

"Listen, you, stay out of my face. Don't you dare stalk me online—"

"What? I'm not *stalking* you," said Kenton, his face red. "I'm just—"

"You back off," said Lauren in a voice so loud that people walking toward their cars stopped to watch. "Keep this up, and I'll see that you never do business again."

Kenton stepped back from the car. "Is that a threat?" he asked, disbelief in his voice.

Lauren thrust her right fist at him, the middle finger extended, before gunning her engine so hard the Jeep leaped ahead, almost hitting an elderly couple crossing to their car.

"That woman is unbelievable," said Kenton as the Jeep drove off.

"She has to be under a lot of stress," said Mallory.

"Stress, hell. She's nuts. Certifiably nuts."

"Kenton, I don't understand why you are so obsessed with that woman," said Mallory as they neared their cars. She had parked next to Osborne. "She obviously wants nothing to do with you."

"It does not make sense," said Kenton. "From the day I met her during the first and only meeting I had with her—nothing has made sense. I know political strategists. I know campaign managers. Nothing about her fits the profile of people working in that field. The first rule in politics is to be *inclusive*, not the opposite. *And* she's paranoid."

"Excuse me, you two," said Osborne, "but what is this 'linked in' that Kenton referred to?"

"It's a social networking website for people in business," said Mallory. "It's international, Dad, millions of people use it."

"It's where you go to recruit people and new business opportunities," said Kenton. "If Lauren Crowell is running a legitimate business as a political consultant or as the head of a small public relations firm, she would be listed." He paused before saying, "I made a reasonable request and got a nutcase response. Maybe it's my old reporter instinct kicking in, but there is one thing I really want to know: Just who the hell is Lauren Crowell?"

"Mallory, let's drive over to the police station. I want to see Chief Ferris about this."

"Hold on, fella," said Osborne. "Better let me call ahead."

Speaking of nut cases, thought Osborne, *the last person Lew might want to see is hothead Kenton.* But to Osborne's surprise, when Lew heard what Kenton wanted, along with Bob Kuhl's concerns, she didn't hesitate.

"Doc, how soon can you get here?"

Chapter Twenty-Two

"Ray is on his way over," said Lew when Osborne arrived with Kenton and Mallory in tow. "He was dropping Kaye Lund off at her home before stopping by his place to pick up that cell phone we hope might be working by now. Bruce should be here any minute, too.

"Hold on, Kenton," she said as Kenton opened his mouth to speak. "I have an interesting piece of news to share with Doc before we get started here."

She looked over at Osborne and said, "Doc, I called your daughter, Erin, this morning. Since she handles a lot of probate, I thought she might point me in the right direction. I wanted to reach the executor of Jane Ericsson's estate to see who her heirs might be. Let me re-phrase that—to see who might profit from Jane's death.

"Bruce had found a copy of her will when he went through her desk, but it's ten years old. The good news is that it did mention which bank handles the investments. Erin was very helpful; she knew just the person who handles estates over there. Sharon

Wright and I talked half an hour ago. Sharon said she helped Jane and her lawyer draw the will up ten years ago, which was not long after her mother died."

Lew gave Kenton and Mallory a severe look. "Please remember, what I am about to say is confidential information. At some point the estate is required to allow public access to the will, but right now I want this information to stay in this room." Mallory and Kenton nodded in agreement.

"Ten years ago, according to Sharon, Jane Ericsson signed a will leaving half her estate, which is substantial, to the Nature Environment Reserve. The other half is to go to Kaye Lund."

"Whoa," said Osborne.

"But," Lew raised one hand, "Jane called the bank three weeks ago to set up a meeting with Sharon and her lawyer to rewrite the will. That meeting was to take place ten days ago. She didn't show. When Sharon called her to reschedule, Jane said she wanted time to think it over."

"So the will has not been changed?" asked Osborne.

"No, right now Kaye Lund stands to inherit nearly ten million dollars. That includes the Ericsson property, and that is valuable timber land."

"That's a good reason to knock someone off," said Kenton with a snort. "I'm sure I would give it some thought."

"Something tells me you would," said Lew, without a smile. "The question I have is whether or not Kaye has been aware of the contents of the will. That, everyone, is the problem. Come in," she said at the sound of knocking on the door.

Ray poked his head in. He was still in his church clothes—carefully pressed khaki pants, a crisp white shirt, and a blue string tie secured at the collar with a brass walleye—and wearing his fish hat with the trout anchored firmly in place. An eager grin stretched across his face as Bruce, who was right behind him, gave Ray's shoulder a shove that bounced Ray into the room.

"Not sure this is the best time for me to welcome a razzbonya with a fish on his head," said Lew. "But come in and sit down, both of you."

"Hat looks terrific," said Mallory with an approving smile as Ray took the chair beside her. "Dad said Kaye fixed it?"

"Yep. Terrific job," said Ray, taking his hat off and placing it with care on the conference table. "But ... that's not the best news, people ... this ... is."

Everyone in the room watched as he pulled Mike Kelly's cell phone from his shirt pocket, stood up, and walked over to set it down in front of Lew. "I thought you might want Bruce in on this, in case he needs more phone repair in the future. I am ... available. As is my ... box of rice." Ray sat back down in the chair, thrust his legs out in front, crossed them at the ankles, folded his arms over his chest, and leaned back.

"I can't stand it when you look so satisfied," said Lew. "Have you tried the phone? Is it working?"

"Yep, yep, and yep. But," said Ray, "what I have not done ... is go through the voicemails on there." He sat up straight, the goofiness gone." I was worried that I might inadvertently delete something."

"Smart move," said Bruce. "Chief Ferris, can we record the voicemails as we listen, just in case they delete automatically after they play?"

"Excuse me, Chief Ferris, do you need us to leave?" asked Mallory. Kenton gave her an annoyed look.

"Yes," said Lew, "please wait outside. I'll call you in when we're finished. Allowing unauthorized people in the vicinity when we're reviewing new evidence could compromise the chain of custody.

Likely not, but I don't want to risk it. Lawyers are great at finding loopholes."

Osborne heard Kenton curse under his breath as they left the room. Before he closed the door behind him, he said, "Don't forget, Chief Ferris, I'm here to report something important, too."

"You're on my list, guy," said Lew. "Please close the door."

The four of them huddled around the conference table as Bruce took the phone, which turned on at the first touch, and got ready to press the voicemail icon. Lew had the recorder going. The first few voicemails were from a woman with a Madison phone number.

"This really is working," said Bruce, his voice low as they listened. "That must be the girlfriend."

Another female voice identified herself as the *New York Times* reporter who said she had received documents he had e-mailed. She also repeated her cell phone number, and said she would be waiting for his call after his meeting with Jane Ericsson.

The next caller identified herself as Jane Ericsson, and said, "Mr. Kelly, I am finally here at my home at the end of Rolf Ericsson Drive. I know it's late, but my flight was delayed by the storm. I'm sorry about this. I realize it's eleven o'clock. If you're available, I'm happy to have you drive over, as I do look forward to our meeting. If you come, I suggest you have the money with you."

That was the last voicemail on the phone. "Is that Jane Ericsson's voice?" Lew asked the room.

"No," said the one person in the room who would absolutely know: the man who had been her lover sixteen years earlier. "That is not Jane Ericsson," said Ray.

"I'd swear that is Lauren Crowell," said Osborne.

Lew checked the digital readout on her recorder and hit a rewind button. Silence. A puzzled look crossed her face. "Doc, this should be the interview we recorded with Lauren Crowell at the Ericsson house Sunday morning. Why don't I have anything?"

"Oh, Lew. I'm sorry," said Osborne, "we had so much going on, I forgot to mention that Lauren picked up your recorder to see what brand it was, and accidentally erased the interview."

"Accidental? Baloney! She did it on purpose. Okay, I'll try this."

She hit more buttons to get a different date, and now the voices of Lauren Crowell, Osborne, and Lewellyn Ferris could be heard.

"She didn't know I had this running during our session yesterday," said Lew. "It's always out of sight when I'm interrogating here in the office."

"That's the woman on Mike Kelly's voicemail," said Bruce. "The one who identifies herself as Jane Ericsson. Sounds the same to my ear, and we can authenticate in the lab."

"Yes, it is," said Lew. "Doc?"

"Without question," said Osborne. "That is Lauren Crowell on Mike Kelly's phone."

"You know what we're missing?" said Lew, looking over at Bruce and Ray. "Jane's phone. But you guys have had no luck finding it, right?"

"Nope," said Bruce. "I took that house and her car apart, too."

"Nothing outdoors that I could find," said Ray.

"On the other hand," said Bruce, "at least this phone has the number we've been searching for. I couldn't find that before—not even staffers in the campaign office had it."

"Can you put a trace on that phone, just like we did with Mike Kelly's?" asked Lew.

"Not yet, not without Jane Ericsson's private access code," said Bruce. "We lucked out with Mike Kelly's because it was an iPhone, and his girlfriend was able to give us his Apple ID."

"Lew, before you bring Kenton back in here," said Osborne, "you need to know what I learned after the memorial service today."

Quickly, he laid out the accountant's concern with the unauthorized withdrawals from the campaign account, and Chuck Winter's comment that Lauren Crowell was not in attendance at the event for donors that he'd hosted in Madison. "Remember, she said she was there," said Osborne.

"I recall that clearly," said Lew. She got up from the conference table and walked over to the door. "Kenton, Mallory, come on in. Kenton, your turn, and make it fast, please."

"I think you should know that Lauren Crowell went off on me in a very, very strange way," said Kenton. "Absolutely bizarre. And Dr. Osborne heard it all. So I'm telling you again that I think it is absolutely mandatory to run a criminal background check on that woman." As if he thought he wasn't being heard, Kenton's voice had risen to a high pitch as he spoke.

"Excellent point, Kenton," said Lew, raising a calming hand. "Dani ran the check through the NCIC this morning. Let's have her tell us what she found."

Lew picked up her phone and asked the switchboard to invite Dani to join them in her office.

"What's the NCIC?" asked Mallory.

"It's the National Crime Information Center," said Bruce. "Only law enforcement people are allowed access to it." Kenton sat silently, his right leg jiggling as they waited for Dani.

"I found an address for one family member, her mother, up in Presque Isle," said Dani, "and hospital records that indicate Lauren has been in and out of psychiatric hospitals for years. She escaped from the last one a year ago and hasn't been seen since.

"I also did a trace on the woman she said she stays with in Madison—Phyllis Cook. I got two names and called them both. Neither one has ever heard of Lauren Crowell."

"So, Kenton," said Lew, "this is still confidential, but you will be happy to hear that because of your experience, Dani's results, and several new developments over the last few hours, that I have requested a warrant for the arrest of Lauren Crowell. I have no doubt that she is a person of interest in the murder of Jane Ericsson."

"Wait," said Bruce, "didn't you tell me that Kaye Lund is the person named in the will as the heir to a chunk of Ericsson money? I understand from Ray here that she is an expert butcher of deer. Shouldn't the Lund woman be interrogated, too?"

"Kaye may be able to butcher a dead animal," said Ray, his voice somber, "but she isn't strong enough to walk much further than from her car to her house. You said yourself that the early report indicates Jane Ericsson suffered a blunt trauma to her head. Kaye doesn't have the strength—"

"Oh, I don't know about that," said Bruce, interrupting. "Adrenaline works in strange ways. Think of the stories you hear of mothers lifting cars off their children after an accident—"

"We'll argue this later," said Lew. "Right now, I want Lauren Crowell in custody."

"If it makes Bruce baby here happy," said Ray, "I'll keep an eye on Kaye Lund. I'll take her some fish later—make sure she's okay. I owe her for the work on my hat."

Ray sounded so sad that Mallory reached over and took his hand. She didn't let go. "Maybe I can help?" she asked.

Chapter Twenty-Three

The warrant for the arrest of Lauren Crowell arrived within an hour. At Lew's request, Osborne drove with her to the Northwoods Inn.

"I'm sorry," said the receptionist at the front desk, "but Ms. Crowell checked out at noon."

"Why am I not surprised," said Lew as they walked back to the cruiser. She called the switchboard. "Marlaine, I want an APB put out for the arrest of Lauren Crowell. Check with Dani for the license plate number and model of the Jeep she's driving. And alert officers that Crowell is a person of interest in a murder. She could be armed. They must approach with caution."

Lew turned to Osborne, "I want to get to Presque Isle ASAP. The mother lives there. She may know where we can find her daughter. If you need to be with Mallory and Kenton—"

"They're big kids," said Osborne. "They can take care of themselves. I'm with you."

"I swear the trees grow taller up here," said Lew, as she and Osborne sped north in her cruiser. When the road was straight, Lew broke the speed limit, but even then it took over an hour to reach Presque Isle. Osborne kept a close eye on the GPS screen tracking the route, which took them off the county highway on to a winding road leading back, back, and back into a densely wooded area.

The road changed from blacktop to gravel. "Someone wants privacy," said Osborne. "I've never been this far out from the main area of Presque Isle." The road looped up and down over a series of hills before ending in front of a large log home. Off to the left was a barn with a Range Rover SUV parked in front of it. Next to that was a Ford 160 pickup.

Off to one side of the large house, Osborne could see water glinting through a stand of birch trees. Aware that there were a thousand lakes in and around Presque Isle, he wondered which one this was.

"Did you call ahead?" asked Osborne as they got out of the cruiser.

"No," said Lew. "Could be a mistake, but we'll see." They walked up to a wide, wooden front door decorated with a carved owl knocker. Lew rang the bell instead.

After a moment's wait, the door swung open. An older woman of medium height with short, wavy gray hair and wearing white slacks with a short-sleeved beige shirt stood in the doorway. "Yes?" she asked, worry flashing across her face when she saw Lew in her uniform. "Something wrong?" Osborne could hear in her tone that she knew the answer to her question.

Judith Barrington held the door open for them to enter. "Follow me," she said, "we'll talk in the den. I've been expecting you. Well, not you in particular, but someone with news of Lauren."

She took a stiff-backed wooden chair next to a desk, and gestured Lew and Osborne to two upholstered chairs across from her.

"Is your husband home?" asked Osborne. "You may want him to hear Chief Ferris's concerns."

"I'm widowed," said the woman. "My husband, Peter, died ten years ago. I have a caretaker who helps me with this place—but I'm afraid it's just me." She gave a soft smile, though her eyes remained serious.

"This may be difficult for you to hear," said Lew, "but your daughter is a suspect in the murder of a woman for whom she was working." She gave a quick sketch of Lauren's role in Jane Ericsson's campaign for the U.S. Senate, and the fact that Jane had been murdered, but stopped short of mentioning the dismemberment of her body.

Judith did not appear surprised. "She's a time bomb," said Judith. "I've been waiting all her life for something like this to happen." She took a deep breath, then said, "I recently learned that my late husband's older sister was committed in her teens for behaviors similar to Lauren's. The family never told anyone, and I only found out when I went to his brother's funeral a couple of months ago."

"You mean there is a family history of mental illness?" asked Lew.

"That's a benign way to put it," said Judith. "Lauren was a difficult child. We were living in Evanston, Illinois, at the time where we could get some counseling. I can't tell you how many types of family counseling and psychiatric testing we went through. Nothing worked. She threw terrible tantrums, broke furniture, brutalized other children. Our dogs were terrified of her. As a child she was like . . . a cancer. She would lie in wait, then strike.

"Maybe we did the wrong thing, but when she was twelve and . . . and I couldn't deal with her any longer, we sent her to school in Switzerland. A psychiatrist there was specializing in treating children like Lauren, so we thought maybe . . ."

"Was she schizophrenic?" asked Lew.

Judith didn't respond. With her right hand, she picked at a thread on her knee. "They diagnosed her as psychotic," she said after a long pause. "But the doctors at the school seemed to think she could be helped, so we kept her there for five years. Then she came back here, and was accepted into a good college out East. She's a very smart woman. It's just that she is disturbed."

As he listened, Osborne could hear in her resigned tone that she had prepared for this conversation for a long, long time. It was as if she was ready for death.

"College lasted three months. One day she was in a minor accident on her bike and was hospitalized in the college infirmary with a concussion. One of the school deans went to get her things from her room, and discovered that Lauren had been stealing from other girls in the dorm. Underwear. Panties, specifically. She had dozens and dozens of pairs of panties. Sounds weird, I know. But that has been one of her patterns: stealing personal items from others.

"It's like . . ." Judith glanced around the room, as if searching there for an answer. "It's like she has always tried to find ways to take on another person's persona. Do you know what I mean? The dean also found disturbing letters that she had been writing to girls in the dorm, threatening letters. And there was promiscuous behavior with several boys that the other girls were dating.

"Needless to say, she was asked to leave. She came home—we were still living in Evanston—and got married to this poor guy, Fred Crowell. He didn't believe me when I tried so hard to warn him off. But they got married, which is where she got her last name. Again, just a few months into that and she went berserk one day. Fred came home and found that she had taken all his personal items and chopped them into tiny, tiny pieces. Socks, shirts, pants, books, his wallet, sports equipment—everything.

"That is when I had her committed to the first of a series of hospitals. But Lauren is crafty. She would bide her time, behaving perfectly until she could escape."

"Would she always come home?" asked Osborne.

"After a while. I never knew exactly when I might see her face in a window—but it was always when she needed money. Meanwhile, shortly before he retired, my husband and I built this place."

"You are really off the beaten track," said Osborne. "This is remote country."

"Maybe we were trying to hide," said Judith. Again the sad smile with serious eyes. "Just before Peter died, I thought we finally had some good news. Lauren was in a psychiatric community in California, where she fell in love with cooking. She became an expert chef, got into organic gardening, artisanal butchering—"

"Butchering?" asked Lew.

"Yes. She has always had a fascination with knives and cutting. I'm afraid poor Fred will vouch for that. By the way, he changed his name after their divorcé. He lives in fear that she'll come after him again."

"But you feel safe up here alone in the woods?" asked Lew.

"Oh, no," said Judith. "You can't see it but I have a security system that covers this house and a four-acre circumference of my property. My caretaker keeps a close eye on the surrounding acres as well. Lauren once set up a tent far enough away that the security system didn't pick it up, so he watches closely, especially since we haven't any idea where she's been for the last year. Once she escaped from that hospital, I cut off the money, too. I've had no idea how she's been surviving."

"Have you asked authorities to search for her?" asked Lew.

"That has never worked. It's one thing to walk away from a psychiatric hospital, quite another to commit a crime. Like I said, Lauren is crafty. After spending close to half a million on private detectives and all, I gave up."

"When was the last time she was home?"

"Several years ago. But a friend told me she thought she saw her just a couple months ago in Manitowish Waters. Browsing galleries. I told her she must have *thought* she saw Lauren, that it was someone else." Judith paused. "If it was Lauren ... that frightens me. Why would she show up around here if she doesn't want to be caught and hospitalized again? It doesn't make sense, but then nothing about my daughter has ever made sense."

"Have you an opinion on what might have set her off?" asked Lew. "She seemed to be very effective in her work as the campaign manager for a woman who trusted her, who gave her a room in her own home."

"I wish I had known, I would have warned someone. As far as what sets her off, I could never predict," said Judith. "Jealousy, maybe. But why did she attack Fred? He loved her. Although he was critical of how she handled their finances. Lauren has been capable of outrageous spending sprees."

"Shoplifting?" asked Lew.

"Oh, yes—that is one of the few times she has been caught," said Judith. "She shoplifts crazy stuff. Things she doesn't need. For her, it's a game."

"Well," said Lew, getting to her feet. "I can't tell you how much I appreciate your candor. If you see or hear from your daughter, please call me immediately. Here is my cell phone number, or call 911 and tell them to reach me."

"And be careful," said Osborne.

"I will. I have been a target for years," said Judith. "I'm also a mother who failed at helping her child. If you are right in thinking that—that Lauren has committed this terrible act—and I believe you are—then I am guilty, too."

She had gotten to their feet and was walking with them to the front door when she stopped. "Be careful when you find her. Lauren's anger is explosive. Be armed and ready. She will steal your soul if she can."

At the door, Lew paused. She put an arm around Judith's shoulders. "I am so sorry that we had to come here today, that we've had to put you through this. I can't begin to imagine how difficult these years have been. I know you've tried your best."

"Thank you," said Judith in a whisper. She pulled the door open and they walked through. As they neared the cruiser, Judith called out, "Wait, Chief Ferris, please wait."

She ran up to them and stood with her arms crossed tight over her chest. "Something I must tell you. I've never told anyone this before, but I think you should know . . . Lauren had a younger sister.

"We were vacationing at Lake Geneva one summer. Lauren was twelve, and Mari just two and a half. The girls were playing in the water at the resort. I asked Lauren to watch Mari while I ran to get something from our room and when I got back . . ." Judith couldn't continue. She dropped her head into her hands and said, "Lauren was holding Mari down under the water. I thought she was reaching for her, but she was holding her down. She drowned my baby."

Judith sobbed. "My fault. I tried to tell Peter what I saw, but he refused to believe me. He made me tell the authorities that Lauren was napping, that I was watching Mari play with sand toys on the beach and left for a short time to get a book that I'd left in the room. When I got back, she had fallen off the dock.

"That's what I swore to. It was not the truth. But Peter did agree with me that she needed help from mental health experts who might understand her. That's when we sent her to Switzerland."

Chapter Twenty-Four

It was still light when Lew dropped Osborne at his car, parked in the police station parking lot. She had checked with the switchboard, but there was no news of a sighting or arrest of Lauren Crowell. Bruce had left a message that he was working with the phone company to see if the phone owned by Jane Ericsson could be traced. So far no luck, as the phone number one of the campaign staffers had turned out to be for an older phone that had been replaced just two weeks ago—and no one had that new number.

Osborne could see the fatigue and worry on Lew's face. He doubted that he looked any better. He knew she would settle in with paperwork that was piling up from the investigation. "Call me if anything breaks, please."

"You know I will," she said. "It's just that I feel so uneasy with this woman on the loose. What if some poor unsuspecting person gets in her way?" Hands on her hips, Lew stared down at the tarmac, thinking.

"What is it?" asked Osborne.

Lew looked up, her dark eyes serious. "Would you mind if I stayed at your place tonight? Last night I had the strangest feeling when I was sitting down by the water that I was being watched. I'm sure it was just a critter—"

"My place it is," said Osborne. "I'll pick up a pizza at the Birchwood Bar on my way home. Take your time here, and we'll eat whenever you're finished."

As he drove home, Osborne couldn't get Kaye out of his thoughts. Even though he was sure she would never have hurt Jane, he didn't like the fact that emotions had reached such a point that Jane had fired Kaye. Nor did it sound good that she stood to inherit half the Ericsson fortune.

What he really didn't like was that Lauren Crowell, emotional instability aside, might be devious enough to make it look like Kaye had motive, opportunity, and the expertise to have dismembered the body. That might be all that would be needed to convince a jury.

Poor Kaye; he wondered how she was doing. Certainly Ray would have stopped by to check on her. He'd said he would.

For no good reason, Osborne suddenly remembered that his shot bag, the one that Mike had chewed on, was still in the back of his car. He had tossed it there right after he and Ray had been at Kaye's early Saturday morning, in hopes that he could drop it off to be repaired on one of his trips to Loon Lake.

Ah, he thought, *just the excuse I need.* He turned onto Rolf Ericsson Drive. He would feel better if he knew Kaye was doing all right. He made a mental note not to say anything about Jane's will, or that Lew had a warrant out for Lauren's arrest. But remembering how Lauren had barged into Kaye's home the day before, he decided it would be wise to share some of what they had learned from Lauren's mother, and encourage Kaye to lock her doors.

He passed the old tennis courts and wound his way past a grove of towering hemlocks. He had just reached the putting green when he saw Kaye's house where it didn't belong: five feet above the tips of the pines in front of him. Airborne. The fiery explosion took less than two seconds but seemed to go on forever, the exterior walls of the old blue house separating before falling back behind the trees.

He hit the accelerator and reached for his phone, braking only long enough to punch in 911.

"Fire!" Osborne was shouting the location when he passed Jane's house and saw the caretaker cottage collapsing in flames. With the phone line still open, he stopped fifty feet from the house. As he jumped from his car, a flaming dervish flew out from what had been the front door.

He grabbed Mike's dog blanket from the back seat and ran. Tackling the burning figure with the blanket, he rolled the body over the ground until he could be sure the flames were extinguished.

"Kaye?" It was Kaye. She was unconscious. He couldn't tell if she was breathing. He felt for a pulse: She was alive. At least for now.

Firemen and an ambulance arrived within moments. Osborne was relieved to let the EMTs take over and rush Kaye to the emergency room. Lew arrived right behind the fire chief. The smoke was so dense, the three of them had to stand far upwind of the burning house. Lew and the fire chief listened while Osborne described what he had seen.

"Dr. Osborne," said the fire chief, "given what you saw driving in, I'm going to bet this was a gas explosion. We'll know more tomorrow." He jogged off to join his team of firemen working their hoses and pulling burning debris from the house.

"Doc, you okay?" asked Lew, rubbing his arm as they stood watching the firemen.

"I think so," said Osborne. "I'm worried sick about Kaye."

"Let me check with the emergency room," said Lew as she pulled out her cell phone.

"We've got her stabilized," said the MD heading up the trauma team. "We're putting her in an ambulance right now and rushing her to our burn unit in Minocqua. I suggest you give them a call in a couple hours. They'll know more then."

"Whew," said Osborne after Lew had clicked off her phone. "At least she's alive. I'm ready to head home. Pizza okay?"

"Pizza sounds perfect," said Lew. "Pizza and sleep."

Chapter Twenty-Five

Osborne wasn't sure who fell asleep first, himself or Lew, but he was sure he hadn't moved a muscle until he heard Mike barking. "What?" asked Lew, drowsy beside him.

"Just the dog," said Osborne, throwing back the coverlet and checking the clock. It was ten minutes before three. "He must hear a raccoon out in the yard. I'll go let him out." As he walked toward the kitchen, Osborne could hear the dog banging against the sides of his crate as he continued to bark.

"Hey, Mike, *no bark*," said Osborne as he reached to unlatch the crate. He had put the dog in his crate so he wouldn't bother Mallory and Kenton in the middle of the night. Osborne was used to the cold nose pressing against his shoulder in the middle of the night, but other people didn't find the affectionate nuzzle quite so comforting. Kenton certainly wouldn't. He opened the back door and was surprised to see the dog take off at run.

A scream ripped the air, and Osborne spun around. *Down-stairs! It came from downstairs.* He ran for the stairway leading to the lower level of his home, nearly colliding with Lew as she came running out of the bedroom.

"What's wrong?"

Another scream, this one guttural as if someone was being strangled. Osborne stumbled down the stairs just as a figure in black ran across the downstairs family room and out the door leading to the patio.

"Mallory? Are you okay?" He reached the bedroom where Mallory had been sleeping. He turned on the light. Mallory was crouched on the floor, holding her head and coughing. "I can't breathe, Dad. Dad, I can't breathe."

"Doc, let me try," said Lew, rushing past him. She knelt beside Mallory and, putting an arm across her back, lifted her up and onto the bed. "Take it slow, Mal, relax . . . good."

Hunched over, Mallory kept making harsh, heaving noises as she tried to get air into her lungs. "Don't try to talk," said Lew. "Just whisper. Take it easy. This happened to me a couple years ago. I know how it feels."

Mallory turned searching eyes on Lew, who said, "I got pinned by this big bruiser of a guy I was trying to arrest. He had me by the throat against my squad car. I know the feeling, but you're getting some air. It's going to be okay. Just try to relax."

"We're here, we'll help you," said Osborne, wondering if he would have to do an emergency tracheotomy. He had never done one, but that didn't mean he couldn't if it meant keeping his daughter alive.

"Lew, should I get a scalpel?" Lew brushed him away with a negative shake of her head.

"Someone—" Mallory squeezed out the word.

"Don't worry about that now, just breathe . . . nice and slow," said Lew.

On his knees beside the bed, Osborne said, "We need you to be okay first." In the distance he could hear the dog snarling, barking. Mike had hold of something—someone.

"Dad, I—" She gagged and coughed.

"Good, Mallory, the coughing is good," said Lew. "You're getting air, just take it easy and don't talk. Was it Kenton? Did you two—"

"No, no . . ." Mallory looked up at the two of them, and that's when Osborne saw the welts on her neck.

Kenton crowded into the room behind Osborne. "Wha-a-a? What's happening?"

After about five minutes, Mallory was able to lean back against the pillows that Lew had propped up behind her. "I'm better," she whispered.

"All right," said Lew, sitting beside her on the bed. "Now tell us what happened."

"I was sound asleep," said Mallory, continuing to whisper. "Had the blanket over my head because there was a mosquito in here and I was too tired to deal with it. All of sudden I felt this pressure on my head and my neck. I heard her say, 'Kenton, this is what happens when you ask too many questions.' At first I couldn't breathe, but I managed to get one knee loose and kick her sideways long enough to scream. Thank heavens you heard me. Then she was on me again—this time with her bare hands. I didn't fight. I tried to pretend that I was unconscious. Dad, that's when she heard you coming down the stairs and she let go. But she punched me hard right in the face."

"I can see," said Osborne. "Afraid you're going to have a black eye, sweetheart."

"Did she break my nose?" Mallory raised a hand to touch herself gingerly.

VICTORIA HOUSTON

"Black eye and a sore neck, but you're alive," said Lew. "You keep saying 'she'—"

"It was that woman, Lauren Crowell," said Mallory. She looked over at Kenton. "She thought I was you until I screamed."

"I am so very sorry," said Kenton, rubbing his forehead. "This is my fault. I thought the woman was a neurotic control freak, not someone who would go this far. My God, Mallory. I don't know what to say."

"I do, and if you'll excuse me, I need to report this," said Lew. "Mallory, we need to get you to the hospital and have you checked out."

"Oh, no, I'll be fine."

"Listen to me, this was attempted murder," said Lew, her voice firm. "I need a detailed report from a physician, and I need it now. Doc, Kenton—do you want to come along?"

"Hell, yes," said Kenton. "Who can sleep after this?"

Before leaving for the hospital, Osborne called for the dog, but Mike was gone. Osborne made sure to leave the gate open.

At three-thirty that morning, the Loon Lake Police switchboard got a 911 call from a man driving home late from a poker game with buddies. He was stopped on County Road C.

"Help! Please. I just hit something crossing the road. I didn't see it till the last minute—it was black and running kind of bent over. I thought I hit a wolf. Got out of my car to make sure it was dead. But, oh my God, it's a woman!"

The caller broke down. "Please send help fast; I think she's dead."

Chapter Twenty-Six

Judith Barrington leaned over the still figure under the sheet in the morgue at St. Mary's Hospital. She had driven down immediately after getting the call from the Loon Lake Police suggesting that she stop first at the police station, where Lew and Osborne were waiting for her. The three of them drove together in Lew's cruiser, parking behind the emergency entrance of the hospital in order to avoid a growing crowd of reporters camped out in the main parking lot.

Osborne and Lew watched in silence as she pulled back the sheet covering her daughter's head. The car had tossed Lauren high in the air upon impact. It was the landing that broke her neck, killing her instantly. The damage to her facial features was so minimal it was difficult to believe she was dead, until you noticed the pallor of her skin.

Judith studied the white face under the fringe of black hair, the mouth agape. An attendant had pressed the eyelids closed. Reaching forward, the mother pushed tendrils of black hair back behind her daughter's ears. "She always liked her hair this way," said Judith. "Even when she was a little girl. She had lovely ears.

"I don't know that I have ever seen her look so peaceful. Funny, I can't help thinking this was what she has always wanted: to be done with us, with life."

"The hard part is she forced someone else to do it for her," said Lew in a quiet voice. "We aren't pressing charges on the driver of the car that hit her. No alcohol was involved. She was wearing black leggings and a long-sleeved black shirt that made it close to impossible to see her in the dark."

"Why was she running across a road in the middle of the night?" asked Judith.

"Doc, you want to answer that?" asked Lew, turning to Osborne.

"Twenty minutes earlier, she entered my home through a lower-level patio door. I happen to have a large black Labrador Retriever who is a good watchdog. Not knowing there was an intruder in the house, I thought he'd heard a raccoon in the yard and let him out of his crate.

"She must have run out through the patio and right into the dog. I'm afraid he nipped her in the calf as he was chasing her, and he wouldn't let her near the car she had parked near my neighbor's driveway. My guess is she thought that if she crossed the highway, she could get away from the dog."

"How bad was the bite? This may sound strange to you," said Judith with a sad smile, "but I need to know everything about how she died." She closed her eyes. "Everything."

"Of course," said Lew. "I lost a child, my son. He was killed in a fight, and I had to see, too. You can't change anything, but it helps to know." Judith nodded.

Osborne raised the sheet from where it covered Lauren Crowell's legs to show where Mike's teeth had broken the skin, leaving traces of blood caked on the shin.

"Umm," said Judith. She reached out to touch the wound, her fingers lingering on the spot. She shook her head. "If only I could have done something over the years to help my Lauren. I could have loved her, you know."

Judith's face was composed and her manner restrained as she said, "The terrible thing is . . . I am so relieved to see her here. To know she can't hurt anyone any more. I feel like I've been let out of prison. Isn't that awful?"

"No," said Lew. "We understand. Your daughter was sick. Not all mental illness can be treated. You said that someone in your husband's family had psychotic episodes and was committed to an institution. That means there may be a genetic factor that you have no control over.

"Mrs. Barrington, if you feel confident that you have made a positive identification of the victim, I believe we're finished here," said Lew. "There's just some paperwork that Dr. Osborne will help you complete, back in my office."

"Not yet," said Judith. "If you don't mind, can we find a place to sit and talk for a few minutes?"

"Of course," said Lew. "The hospital has a visitor center with some private rooms. Let's walk down there."

Judith followed them down the hall to a small room. After closing the door behind her, she set her purse on a side table and sat down, her hands clasped in her lap. Osborne found a quiet elegance in her composure.

"I'm so worried about the people that Lauren has hurt. Dr. Osborne, how is your daughter? Chief Ferris told me that Lauren assaulted—"

"She's going to be fine. Bruised, yes, and pretty shaken, but she'll be fine."

He saw no point in burdening the poor woman with more details than were necessary. And Mallory was doing okay. The trauma physician found no bruising inside the throat, nothing torn or broken in spite of the initial pain from the pressure on her neck. The black eye should be gone in a week.

"But the other woman, the one who was so terribly burned when her house exploded. Chief Ferris, didn't you say that the report from the fire department was that someone had turned on all the burners on the gas stove in that old house?"

"Yes," said Lew. "We'll never prove it, but since Dr. Osborne was there two days ago when Lauren barged into the house without knocking, angry that Kaye was planning a memorial service for Jane Ericsson, I am convinced she snuck in and turned on the gas—possibly while Kaye was asleep. Kaye has a habit of taking long naps in her rocking chair. With the amount of gas that had filled that house, all that was needed was a tiny spark from a move as simple as pressing the latch on the screen door—"

"Or moving the rocking chair," said Osborne. "Kaye is not senile, so it is highly unlikely she turned on the gas jets herself."

"Will she die?" asked Judith.

"No," said Osborne, "I checked with the MDs in the burn unit where she is being treated, and the good news is that she has stabilized. She will need skin grafts and there will be some scarring, but they expect her to recover. Kaye has many friends who are willing to help, so the prognosis is good—not great, but good. Does that help?"

"Yes, a great deal. Chief Ferris, you must have questions for me," said Judith. "If not now, eventually, so please don't hesitate to get in touch."

"I do, but I am not sure you are up for answering them at the moment," said Lew. "Try me," said Judith. "The more we know, the more we can put behind us."

"I have two questions," said Lew, pausing before she continued. "The big one is why Lauren would have turned on Jane Ericsson. Jane trusted her. Based on what the other staff people on the campaign say, she seems to have admired Lauren. She was paying her well . . ."

"Jane Ericsson must have said 'no' to something," said Judith. "Something important to Lauren. It's the 'no' that sets her off."

"We think that Lauren had almost convinced Jane to include her in her will," said Lew. "To rewrite the will: to remove Kaye Lund, whom Jane had known since childhood, and add Lauren."

"Something else, Chief Ferris," said Osborne. "We know she was siphoning funds from the campaign. Could Jane have confronted her on that?"

"To expect to get away with either doesn't make a lot of sense," said Lew. "Although she could have escaped with the money, I guess. We know she has several hundred thousand hidden somewhere."

"You think reality meant anything to Lauren?" asked Judith. It was a rhetorical question. "She lived in her own world, a fantasy world where she got what she wanted, or else."

"But why the cutting? Why dismember the body?" asked Lew.

"She did that before. Remember I told you she cut up all of her ex-husband's personal clothing? I didn't mention that after her little sister's death, I found clothing of Mari's cut up and hidden. It was Lauren's way of making what troubled her disappear."

"She could say that Jane had disappeared after an alcoholic binge," said Osborne. "Maybe fallen off the proverbial dock and never seen again. Happens up here."

"Dr. Osborne has a point," said Lew. "It was only by a stroke of luck that the utility worker spotted those bundles in the midst of the storm and flooding. If he hadn't thought he was seeing someone's prize venison roasts, we could still be searching for a missing candidate for the U.S. Senate.

"Something that occurs to me is how much media attention this has gotten. In a funny way, it's possible that Lauren could have stepped into Jane's shoes—not run for office, but certainly be the focus of attention nationwide."

"I told you she could steal your soul. She did her best to steal mine."

"But the murder of Mike Kelly confounds me," said Lew. "We know she did it, because she had Jane's phone in her car. We found the phone this morning. And we know it was her voice on that victim's voicemail that lured him to Jane's house. Would she have killed him for fifty thousand dollars?"

"I wouldn't be surprised," said Judith. "I believe I told you I cut her off the minute she escaped from that psychiatric hospital. I don't know what she's been living on since."

"Then why not dismember Mike Kelly's body, too?"

"Not the same. She wanted the money. She may not have liked that person, but she wouldn't have fixated on him like she did with this Ericsson woman. You know, it surprises me that Jane Ericsson didn't see something off-kilter in Lauren's behavior."

"Not me," said Osborne. "I knew her father and mother. People like the Ericssons, who are handsome individuals born into prestige and money, tend to be sloppy in their interactions with others. They assume the people who work for them will do whatever they're told. They assume a natural authority, and don't care to be bothered with 'little' stuff. I'm under the impression that Lauren did a very good job controlling everything for Jane—even covering up for her binge drinking."

"Last question, Judith," said Lew. "Regarding the murder and dismemberment of Jane Ericsson—do you think she planned ahead?"

Judith closed her eyes and shook her head. "Honestly, Chief Ferris—how on earth would I know? I'm no psychopath."

Chapter Twenty-Seven

By late Friday afternoon, media interest in the Ericsson murder had waned, and Lew felt comfortable taking the afternoon off. Earlier that morning Osborne had said good-bye to Mallory and Kenton as they headed off to Chicago, two days later than they had planned.

Now, with afternoon temperatures balmy in the low eighties, it was decided that the dock at Osborne's would be the place to recuperate.

"Bruce," said Lew, stopping by the conference room where Bruce had set up his temporary headquarters. "After you finish those reports, would you like to join Doc and myself out at his place? We expect Ray to drop by when he's back from checking on Kaye."

She did not have to twist Bruce's arm.

The afternoon was classic northern Wisconsin in the summertime: the lake sparkling as if someone had laid a cloak of diamonds across gentle waves, the sky overhead a brilliant blue, and not even the whine of a jet ski to mar the peace.

Anxious to get out of her uniform and unload her holsters—one each for the gun, the cell phone, and the walkie-talkie—Lew had rushed to pull on her favorite black and white striped swimsuit. Once on the lounge chair, she pulled a wide-brimmed straw hat down over her eyes and settled back to let the sunlight and an easy breeze wash away the stress of the past week.

Osborne lay next to her. He wore a scruffy pair of Bermuda shorts that were at least twenty years old, and a faded red T-shirt dating back to his dental school days. It was an outfit that Mary Lee had banned, so he had crammed the shorts and shirt into a file drawer in the secret office that he had managed to shoe-horn into a small space behind the garage porch, an area he'd been allotted for cleaning fish and fowl. An area Mary Lee had avoided.

On one of Lew's first visits to his place, Osborne had tested out her response to his crummy shorts and shirt. She hadn't blinked. "Don't you look comfy, Doc? How the hell long have you owned those?" His confession had made her laugh.

With Lew and Osborne relaxing on the two lounge chairs, Bruce plopped himself into one of four green Adirondack chairs lined up to face west. Cell phone to his ear, he fielded a call from one of his colleagues at the Wausau Crime Lab, who was wondering when he would return. He, too, was basking in shorts, but they were hidden under an oversized Hawaiian shirt destined to frighten any fish approaching the dock, at least according to Lew.

"Tell them Monday," said Lew, overhearing his conversation and speaking from under her hat. "They're just jealous 'cause you were interviewed on the national evening news." She pushed the hat up and glanced over at Bruce. "Seriously, I owe you some time on muskie water. How about tomorrow morning before it gets too hot?"

"You got it," said Bruce. "Tomorrow's Saturday. I don't need an excuse."

"All righty, then," said Lew. "We have a plan." And she pulled the hat back down over her eyes.

The only occupant on the dock not wearing shorts was the dog. On returning from the morgue after Judith Barrington identified her daughter, Osborne had been worried about Mike. When leaving the house to rush Mallory to the hospital after she was attacked, he had made sure to leave the yard gate open, hoping the black Lab would find his way home. To Osborne's great relief, the dog showed up later that day. He was hungry and covered with burrs, but otherwise unscathed.

A quick, happy bark from Mike, who was curled up at Osborne's feet, signaled Ray's arrival. Ray, skipping down the stone walkway to the dock, was resplendent in khaki shorts and a fishing shirt, sleeves rolled up, to match. The repaired hat with its reinvigorated stuffed trout was stuck firmly on his head.

"Hey, look what I caught coming through the rye . . ."

"Coming through Loon Lake, you mean," said Christina, taking the stone stairs two at a time behind Ray.

"She's brought photos of the vending machines her old man is helping me buy," said Ray.

"Tell us about Kaye first," said Osborne, straightening up in his chair. "How's she doing?"

"She is looking swell," said Ray. "The bandages on her arms and face have come off. She's healing nicely. But the great news is she got the call from the executor on Jane Ericsson's estate. Yesterday. She . . . cannot . . . believe it. She is beside herself."

"I'm sure she never expected to be named in the will," said Lew. She sat up as she said, "Ray, I'm curious. Do you think Lauren was telling the truth when she said that Kaye had threatened to blackmail Jane regarding that affair you two had?"

"What?" asked Christina, her eyes wide as she threw a questioning look at Ray.

"Tell you about it later," said Ray, raising a finger to his lips and hoping Lew would get the hint. "But to answer your question, Chief: I asked Kaye about that. I found it hard to believe she would do any such thing.

"Kaye said she never asked for money to keep quiet. What she *did* do—and she's not proud of it—is when Jane told her she was fired, Kaye threw the affair in her face. She said something to the effect of, 'You think you're perfect, you think you got the race nailed—I could do you a lot of damage if I wanted to.'

"But she did not, absolutely did not, make any mention of keeping her mouth shut for money. And I believe her."

"You have got to tell me more," said Christina. "What is this affair you people are talking about?"

"I will, I will—later," said Ray, rolling his eyes.

Bruce chuckled. "Hey, hope you blog it, bud," he said, and got a dark look.

"She must be thrilled to be inheriting all that money and the land," said Osborne. "Suddenly Kaye is a rich woman, as rich as Jane Ericsson was."

"Richer," said Lew. "Kaye may not be perfect, but she has a good heart."

"And she has a plan for the money," said Ray. "She wants to turn Jane's new house into an environmental lab open to the public, call it the Ericsson-Lund Natural Resources Center. She wants it to be a place for research and classes about managing and preserving that old growth hemlock forest, as well as other northern Wisconsin natural resources. She's just starting to think about it."

"I should talk to her," said Bruce. "I have some scientist friends who might be interested."

"She wants to preserve trees, not dead bodies," said Ray.

"Come on, you know what I mean."

"Hey, can I show you these?" asked Ray, eager to change the subject. "Look." He laid out six photos of different vending machines. "We're going to start with three and see how it goes. Christina's father is putting up the initial investment, but I have to pay him back half of that once the business is rolling."

After a quick study of the photos, Osborne asked, "Do any of these come with a backup generator, or battery pack of some kind?"

"Yes, this one," said Ray, pointing. "That's the one we like, too."

"And you'll have all three of these installed in this area?" asked Lew.

"Yep. Starting next May, with opening fishing season."

"Chief Ferris, I have a question," said Christina. "I was here when those body parts were found. Have any more surfaced?"

"Thank you for ruining my afternoon," said Lew. She sat up, setting her sun hat aside, and reached for a glass of iced tea. "The answer is no. Not yet. My nightmare is that some youngster out fishing this fall or next spring is going to hook one of those bundles that made it into the Tomorrow River and . . ."

"And?" asked Bruce, his eyebrows bouncing with delight.

"We'll hear the scream all the way in Loon Lake, is what will happen. We'll have to put the poor kid in therapy," said Lew with a laugh. "Jeez Louise, I hope and pray that what remains of poor Jane Ericsson rests forever at the bottom of the Tomorrow River."

"How 'bout the money?" asked Ray. "Any luck finding where that has been stashed?"

"This is the last we discuss this case today, agreed?" said Lew. "I want my weekend off. So the final word on the money issue is this: Dani did a search of gas and electricity accounts through Wisconsin Public Service, and found that Lauren had an account. She used her own name to get approved for service to a small cabin up in Manitowish Waters. Todd searched it this morning and found cash, cashier's checks, and a one-way plane ticket to Barbados. The woman had plans. But to answer your question— yes, I think we've found all the money."

"If she had a place in Manitowish Waters, I'm convinced she did try to steal those hair extensions from my gallery," said Christina.

Osborne perked up. "Like Kenton said: it's a person's bad habits that give them away. Lauren's mother said she had been caught shoplifting more than once."

"Speaking of Kenton," said Ray, "will Mallory be inviting him back?"

"Har-de-har-har," said Osborne, dismissing the subject. "Would you and Christina like to sit down and have an iced tea?"

"Thanks, Doc. We have plans," said Ray. "Bruce, come join us for fish fry—these two need a break from us. Right?" Osborne and Lew just smiled.

When they had gone, Osborne turned sideways on his lounge chair. It wasn't often that he got to enjoy seeing Lew in her swimsuit. Her figure was stalwart, her breasts firm and inviting: a promise of the pleasant evening ahead.